Lucy felt a **uncertainty** **when she tho** **of a job to a man she'd only met briefly over a dinner table.**

It had all been done quickly and impulsively—with hindsight perhaps she should have taken more time to make up her mind. But Callum had such an engaging personality and persuasive manner that she'd allowed her normal caution to fly to the wind.

No good worrying now about whether Callum would fit in—they'd just have to rub along together for at least three months!

Judy Campbell is from Cheshire. As a teenager she spent a great year at high school in Oregon, USA, as an exchange student. She has worked in a variety of jobs, including teaching young children, being a secretary and running a small family business. Her husband comes from a medical family, and one of their three grown-up children is a GP. Any spare time—when she's not writing romantic fiction—is spent playing golf, especially in the Highlands of Scotland.

Recent titles by the same author:

DATING DR CARTER
THE BACHELOR DOCTOR
TEMPTING DR TEMPLETON
A HUSBAND TO TRUST

THE DOCTOR'S
SECRET BABY

BY
JUDY CAMPBELL

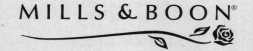

First published in Great Britain 2003
Harlequin Mills & Boon Limited,
Eton House, 18-24 Paradise Road, Richmond, Surrey TW9 1SR

© Judy Campbell 2003

ISBN 0 263 83474 3

Set in Times Roman 10½ on 12 pt.
03-1003-47972

Printed and bound in Spain
by Litografía Rosés, S.A., Barcelona

CHAPTER ONE

SO THIS was the 'informal' supper party her sister had insisted on holding for her! Lucy Cunningham cast an amused look at the beautifully decorated table with an exquisite floral arrangement of summer flowers in the table centre. It was set with the very best of china, sparkling crystal and linen—nothing out of place and certainly looking anything but a casual last-minute arrangement. The room was like the stage set for a sophisticated play, French windows opening onto a pretty little courtyard, and the soft scent of sweet peas wafting in on the balmy night air.

Typical of Jan that she could entertain with such consummate ease and still manage to look unflustered and as elegant as ever! Lucy watched her sister in the clinging cream sheath dress deftly serve the food whilst joining in the conversation, and reflected wryly that her own entertaining skills seemed to result in minor chaos everywhere—especially in the kitchen, and her look was more frazzled than glamorous after a cooking session. No, Jan certainly couldn't be faulted on any matter of decor or the serving of delicious food—everything was perfection.

When it came to guests, however... Lucy's eyes strayed round the table and looked at Jan's friends. It was lovely of her sister to hold a birthday dinner for her, but perhaps she would have felt more comfortable with a quiet family party. These people had the witty repartee and slightly superficial air of London society—she felt she had little in common with them, perhaps because she didn't know them. They were very different to the down-to-earth country folk she lived and worked among.

She flicked a sardonic eye over the portly young stockbroker at the end of the table, the earnest solicitor sitting opposite her and, of course, her own brother-in-law, Max, a brilliantly successful barrister married to her sister Jan, an equally successful actress. They were accompanied by their wives, glittering and sophisticated, and wearing, Lucy was sure, extremely expensive clothes. It was not that she disliked these people or, indeed, that they were nasty: it was just that her world and theirs were a million miles apart. It looked, she thought ruefully, as if she was in for rather a boring evening!

There was only one single man there, who was back in England after working in Australia, the brother of the solicitor. He was sitting next to her and hadn't said much beyond a polite 'Good evening' when introduced. Now he was listening to the others making animated conversation about the latest diet, which involved a strict detoxification regime for two weeks.

The stockbroker leant forward in his chair and addressed Lucy. 'Now, you're a doctor,' he drawled. 'What's your opinion? Do you think it's a good idea to deny yourself the basics of life such as food and drink for a hideously long time in order to look like a stick insect?'

His wife giggled. 'You know it's a good idea, Archie…you just have no will-power. His doctor's told him he's got to lose two stone.'

Archie growled crossly. 'I'm going to change my

doctor—he's always telling me off.' He turned to Lucy. 'I'd ask to be put on your list only you're up in the wilds of Scotland somewhere, aren't you?'

'That's right...a country practice. It's very beautiful.'

'But Lucy's completely buried away—one might as well live on the moon for all the fun she can get. I'm afraid she's only interested in her work.' Mrs Cunningham, Lucy's mother, spoke from the doorway. She bore a magnificent fruit meringue concoction in her hands, and looked fretfully at her daughter. 'When I think what a life she could have here in London, and the people she could meet...well, it seems such a waste to work in the back of beyond when you could have the best of both worlds here!'

Lucy sighed—her mother lived with Jan her sister and was also at the dinner party. She should have been used by now to the barbed comments Mrs Cunningham made about her, the constant comparisons between her and the life and style that Jan led— but it still rankled.

'You know I love it up there, Mother,' she protested. 'It's a wonderful life—the traffic's light, the country air is fantastic and the people are great...'

'Nonsense!' said Mrs Cunningham firmly. 'The day you left London you abandoned all hope of meeting like-minded people.'

For 'like-minded' read 'suitable husband', thought Lucy, scowling at her reflection in the mirror behind the solicitor's head. That seemed to be her mother's ambition for her—to marry a well-connected and wealthy man and forget about her career and the hard work that had led up to it. Jan had managed both— her mother was proud of her other daughter's fame and the way she combined her exciting stage and film roles with that of glamorous mother. But Mrs Cunningham seemed to be most proud of Jan's marriage to Max Balfour, a highly successful barrister who would undoubtedly become a judge some day.

Lucy sighed ruefully—she wasn't the marrying kind, was she? She was very careful to steer clear of relationships after bitter experience had shown that men had a habit of disappearing out of her life. She wasn't going to be sidetracked by allowing herself to have hopeless yearnings for romance again—better to concentrate on the work she loved.

'I've plenty of congenial friends in Ballachter—' she began defiantly.

Her mother ignored her remark and said crisply, 'I just wish, Jan, you could take your little sister in hand and get her some decent clothes while she's here—she could be so attractive if she tried to make something of herself. Lucy used to have such beautiful long black hair—it's a shame she cut it so short!' She sighed heavily. 'Of course, she always was rather a tomboy!'

Lucy was silent, her cheeks burning with irritation, but inside she was longing to spit out, I'm only what you made me, Mother!

No good standing up to her mother, however—it would only end in the guests being more embarrassed than they were already. When she got into her stride, Mrs Cunningham didn't seem to mind what she said… Lucy looked down at her plate and bit her lip. Her mother hadn't had an easy life and perhaps it was understandable that because of her unhappiness she had become sharper and more critical over the years. There were reasons for it, but it still hurt that she could never be the daughter her mother wanted her to be.

Jan shot Lucy a sympathetic look—she was aware how critical their mother was of Lucy and tried to protect her from the worst of her remarks.

'Mum,' she said reprovingly, 'you know Lucy looks wonderful—if only we could all look as young as she does with that heavenly complexion! I think we should all raise our glasses to my darling sister. Happy birthday, Lucy—so glad your meeting brought you to London at the right time! It's been too long since we've seen you.'

Everyone murmured politely, toasting Lucy's health, and the conversation drifted mercifully away from the subject of Lucy and her lifestyle and looks. Thank God, she thought, taking a long sip of Max's excellent red wine, I shall be away from here tomorrow and back in the Highlands, able to be myself again. She loved her mother despite her outbursts, but after three days in her company both had begun to get on each other's nerves—and perhaps that was why she had ended up living nearly five hundred miles away.

'So you're a doctor, are you?'

The deep quiet voice beside Lucy made her jump. She hadn't taken much notice of the solicitor's brother sitting beside her—had even forgotten his name. She looked at him properly for the first time and felt a flicker of surprise at the startlingly attractive face that looked back at her—deep blue eyes were set in a tanned face and tousled auburn hair fringed his forehead. No doubt he was in the acting profession like her sister and so many of her friends, and probably very aware of his devastatingly handsome looks and how most of the female population would react to him!

'Yes, I'm in general practice,' she replied, dragging her gaze away from his good-looking face and noting with amusement that he was dressed in a much more casual manner, in his multi-patterned cotton shirt over faded blue jeans, than the other, dinner-jacketed men. With an inward giggle Lucy could almost feel the steely looks of disapproval her mother kept casting in his direction—she hated people to be unconventional.

The man's eyes twinkled. 'And is your mother right—that you're a career-woman?'

For some reason the question irritated Lucy—the expression made her seem hard, only interested in herself and her own life. 'No harm in that, is there?' she said rather defensively. 'Is it wrong to have a bit of ambition?'

The man flicked a quick look at her, as if aware he'd touched a nerve. 'Not at all,' he said lightly, 'I admire people who are single-minded and use their skills to the best of their ability.' The amazing blue eyes looked appealingly at her. 'Forgive me—I ask too many questions. A bad habit of mine... I don't mean to pry.'

His smile was apologetic and rather endearing, and Lucy softened. Perhaps she was being a little tetchy, but London always seemed to have that effect on her. She made an effort to be more outgoing, and explained, 'I came up to London for a meeting and to interview one or two people for a vacancy in our practice. We had a few replies from this area, so it seemed a good idea to see them whilst I was here.'

'And was there anyone suitable?'

Lucy shook her head. 'Not really—we need someone with experience and who doesn't mind working in a practice with patients scattered over a large rural area. Most of the people I saw cooled off rapidly when they realised just how remote our practice is—and the workload they'd be expected to undertake.'

'So what will you do?'

She smiled ruefully. 'Rely on the locums we've been using since the previous partner left—but they're mostly elderly retired GPs and not keen on doing visits or having long surgeries.'

His look was sympathetic. 'I imagine you've been taking the brunt of it, then?'

Lucy's attention wandered slightly, noting the green flecks in the remarkable blue eyes and the dark lashes fringing them—quite unusual, she reflected. The kind of eyes you looked at twice, the kind of eyes you found yourself gazing at... Then she realised that the man was waiting for a reply and pulled herself together irritably, curiously annoyed with herself for noticing anything about his physical attributes. What had he just asked her? She forced herself back into the present.

'Er, yes, I have been working hard—it's been pretty desperate really. The sooner we have an enthusiastic permanent person, the better...' She sighed. 'No wonder I've no time to have wonderful hairdos or to go shopping for designer clothes...even if I lived near exclusive shops.'

The man chuckled, a cheery light-hearted sound, and his glance lingered on her face for a second. 'I like your hair as it is,' he said decisively. 'It looks rather gamine-like to me—suits the shape of your face and emphasises those big eyes of yours. I should keep it like it is, Lucy!' There was a pause and then he added softly, 'And I think your sister's quite right—you have got a lovely complexion!'

For a second Lucy felt a ridiculous sense of elation at his compliment, then she suppressed the feeling crossly. These good-looking men were all the same, weren't they? They threw out compliments like confetti, and she sure wasn't going to react to that. The flattering comments men sometimes came up with were just that—flattery, and she knew enough of Jan's 'luvvie' friends with their gushing phrases to know they didn't mean anything. Annoying though her mother was, at least she spoke the truth when she said that she, Lucy, didn't make the most of herself.

She looked at him coolly. 'Please! Don't start giving me these old chat-up lines!'

The man grinned, unabashed. 'You don't have to believe me, but I assure you I only give compliments when I mean them!'

The amazing eyes locked onto hers like laser beams, and she looked away, slightly embarrassed, aware of an unusual fluttering sensation somewhere in the pit of her stomach.

'Thank you,' she said stiffly. 'I guess I'm not used to being called gamine-like!'

He looked at Jan and then back at Lucy. 'You're not very like your sister in looks—she's very fair and not as tall as you are.'

She smiled wanly—most people ended up comparing them, Jan's petite figure against her tall athletic physique. Sometimes Lucy felt when they were standing together that she looked like a stately battleship next to a small yacht!

'I'm supposed to take after my father. I'm afraid I could never compare to Jan's glamorous looks or her talents. Our interests are quite different, too, of course—she has a family and a career.'

'And you don't have a family?'

'No,' Lucy said rather shortly. She placed her knife and fork very precisely on her plate. 'I'm busy enough as it is…and, as I said before, I love my work.'

'Then you're a fortunate woman. So many people plod through life disliking their jobs—it's just a means to an end.'

Lucy softened again towards him—at least he was more interested in her than the other guests.

'I'm afraid I didn't catch your name. I know you're Paul's brother, that's all, and that you've come back from abroad.'

He smiled. 'I'm Callum Tate. I'm staying with Paul for a few days until I find myself a job again—hopefully that won't be too long. I'm lucky that there's no shortage of jobs in my line.'

Lucy was surprised. She'd always thought the acting profession was rather precarious, although perhaps with his looks he could afford to be fairly confident.

'Have you just finished a good run?'

Callum looked puzzled. 'A good run? Do you mean as in keeping fit?'

'No, no, I mean in the theatre—that's what you do, isn't it?'

Amused blue eyes twinkled at her. 'No—if I'm at the theatre I'm definitely part of the audience.'

'Oh, sorry, I thought you were an actor,' Lucy said, feeling rather foolish.

'Now, what made you think that?' he said with a grin.

'Because...' Lucy's voice trailed off and her cheeks reddened. She was certainly not going to say that she'd assumed he was an actor because he was so good-looking! 'Because Jan has so many friends in the acting profession,' she finished quickly. She changed the subject adroitly. 'So what do you actually do?'

'As it happens, I'm also a medic—a GP actually— and, as I said, looking for work.'

'That should be easy in London—there's a shortage of GPs.'

'Oh, I don't want to work here,' he replied. He looked at her with a slight smile and raised an eyebrow. 'Any chance of a job up in Ballachter?'

'Are you being serious?'

'Sure I am—it sounds a great place.'

The cheek of the man! Lucy looked coldly at the blue eyes that danced at her, and tried to ignore a sudden inexplicable and disturbing thumping of her heart. 'I know nothing about you,' she said loftily.

He leaned towards her, his gaze holding hers persuasively. Lucy felt her heart go into overdrive—he had a very engaging look. 'I can tell you everything you want to know,' he said softly.

Lucy pushed his engaging looks firmly to the back of her consciousness. 'But you know nothing about the job—it might not suit you. There's a lot of hard work—I'm the full-time partner and I have a part-time salaried partner who wants to retire as he's not very well, but the practice is spread over a large area.'

He shrugged. 'I'm not afraid of hard work. It was only a suggestion, of course. The thing is, you're looking for a doctor and I'm looking for a job—and

I like the thought of a country practice. I'm used to working in the wilds—prefer it, in fact.'

'And just how much experience have you had?'

Callum Tate grinned. 'No good being modest! I've dealt with practically everything in the book except open heart and brain surgery. When it comes to small ops, I'm your man—and as for dealing with children and the elderly, I'm nothing short of expert!'

Lucy couldn't help laughing. 'And where did you get all this fantastic experience?'

'In the Australian outback. I joined the Flying Doctor Service for two years, and loved every moment of it. I don't like big cities—never have. It was an exciting and fulfilling life.'

Lucy frowned. 'Then what made you come back here if you enjoyed it so much in Australia?'

Callum picked up his glass and swirled the red wine around for a second before taking a deep sip, the pleasant planes of his face suddenly hardening.

'Oh, circumstances change, you know… That part of my life is over now. It was a wonderful challenge but I didn't want to stay there for ever—after all, my roots are here.'

Lucy looked at him thoughtfully. Was his tone just a little too casual and airy? She felt she'd touched a raw nerve, and wondered if there was a hidden agenda in Callum Tate's history. She couldn't believe that a man like him wasn't married or at least have a partner. If he wanted a job, she felt she had the right to ask him.

'You didn't put roots down in Australia, then? No family while you were there?'

Was there a hint of bitterness in his curt reply? 'Just an ex-wife, that's all. And she very definitely didn't want to come back with me—so I've no one to think of but myself now.'

'I'm sorry,' murmured Lucy rather inadequately. 'That must be difficult for you.'

'Oh, don't worry—it's all history.' He spoke firmly, as if closing the subject. 'I'm ready to begin the rest of my life now.'

Still waters run deep, reflected Lucy. Callum Tate wasn't just a good-looking charmer—he'd had sadness in his life which she guessed had left scars. On the face of it however, he seemed the answer to a prayer—enthusiastic, lots of relevant experience and happy to work in a remote place. She ought to grab him with both hands.

'Do you have references from your last employment?'

'Of course, and the phone number and email address of my boss in Woolaterra where I was based. He was a great guy to work with—really laid back.'

'Really?' Lucy's tone was rather prim. 'I'm afraid I don't like to be too casual at work. I'm very organised, like things to be just so. If you're used to that sort of approach we might not suit each other.'

His eyes twinkled into hers. 'I guess I could live up to your standards—laid back doesn't necessarily mean incompetent, you know. I think I've saved more patients than killed them.'

Lucy looked abashed. 'Look, I didn't mean to imply that you weren't up to the job. It's just that it's a big thing, coming up to Ballachter and finding out that we may be more, well, formal than you were in Australia. You might not like that.'

'We could always give it a go,' replied Callum lightly.

Lucy played with her knife and fork silently for a second. The Ballachter practice needed someone urgently but she didn't want to make a mistake and land Robert, her partner, and herself with another problem. The last partner had left under a cloud and what they needed was stability in the practice before Robert finally retired. Callum's offer had rather taken her off guard—she liked to read people's CVs carefully before interviews, size them up when she met them. Callum Tate seemed impetuous, and she needed time to assess him. She wasn't going to be bounced into taking someone on just because she was desperate—after all, she would have to work closely with the man.

As if reading her thoughts, he smiled gently at her. 'You're right to be cautious—no good being stuck with someone you can't stand. We'd probably have a three-month trial period anyway.'

Lucy nodded, and reflected that after all she didn't really have much to lose if she did take Callum on. It would be such a relief to go back home tomorrow knowing that she had finally settled on someone. It was just... She shot a look under her lashes at him, trying to decide why it was she had such reservations—the man seemed almost perfect. Perhaps that was it—he was like some dishy actor playing the part of a doctor, every woman's idea of a star—but just how competent was he? She only had his bland words assuring her that he was good at his job. Normally at an interview she would already be armed with the candidate's references and CV—would it be right to take a gamble and offer him a job?

Archie's booming voice from the other end of the table interrupted her thoughts. 'You two getting to know each other, I see. You'll have a lot in common, both being doctors. But you be careful of Callum, Lucy. Lord knows what he got up to in Australia, although I do know he could tell you a tale or two.'

'I was just telling Lucy about my life over there,' said Callum easily, 'and the experiences I had in the outback.'

Archie had evidently had a lot to drink. He wagged a knowing finger at Callum. 'I bet you've had all kinds of experiences—I know you medics! I try and darken their doors as little as I can!'

He took a large forkful of food and stuffed it into his mouth, laughing uproariously at his own wit, others joining in. That was why it was so extraordinary when suddenly his laughter stopped on a high-pitched note. The chatter died down as people looked at him enquiringly, then he clutched his throat, opening and shutting his mouth with no sound coming out. For a moment nobody moved, staring at him rather uncomfortably, then he leant forward on his chair, his face purpling and his eyes protruding, still making no noise.

His wife gave an uncertain laugh. 'What on earth are you doing? You all right, Archie?' she asked nervously. 'You're not acting the fool, are you?'

Archie made no reply, and Lucy's mother gave a gasp of horror, one hand going to her mouth. Then there was a scraping noise as Callum pushed back his chair and moved swiftly towards Archie, whose hands were plucking vainly at his collar.

'He's choking,' said Callum tersely. 'We've got to remove the obstruction. Help me lift him up Max.' His voice was urgent and commanding. 'I've got to get my arms round him... Quick—lift him. *Now!*'

Archie was a big man but they managed to heave him to his feet, the man still strangely silent, his arms flailing. Callum bent him forward and, placing one fist under Archie's breastbone, grasped his wrist with the other hand. Then he made a quick hard, thrusting movement inwards and upwards. Nothing happened. Archie's face was still purple, his body sagging against Callum. Little cries of distress came from round the table as they watched Callum desperately trying to help the man. He repeated the procedure and suddenly, like a bullet from a gun, a piece of meat shot across the table from the victim's mouth. There was a gasping sound and a spluttering cough, then a series of hoarse ragged intakes of breath. Archie collapsed back on the chair, his face changing from deep red to ashen, his eyes closed.

A stunned silence followed in the room, then an outburst of hysterical chatter.

'My God...what the hell happened, man?' asked Max. The episode had taken only a minute or two, but the drama of the whole thing seemed to have taken place almost in slow motion.

'What happened was that Archie was choking,' said Lucy in a quiet voice. 'We can thank Callum for saving his life. If he hadn't been so quick in realising that Archie's windpipe was completely obstructed so that he couldn't breathe at all, this might have ended very differently!'

She looked across at Callum, lounging casually against a chair and looking no more fazed than if he had just put a plaster over a cut. Probably only he and she knew just what a close call Archie had had. Pretty impressive, Dr Tate, she reflected. She handed a glass of water to the perspiring, white-faced Archie.

'You're lucky Callum was here,' she said. 'I doubt I'd have had the strength to do the Heimlich manoeuvre on a man your size.'

Archie sipped the water, then sat back exhausted in his chair. 'That was too close for comfort,' he murmured. He opened his eyes and looked rather sheepishly at Callum. 'Thanks, old man...I owe you one. I certainly wouldn't want to go through that again.'

Callum patted Archie on the arm. 'Glad to be of service,' he murmured. He looked around at the other guests, their faces still shocked after the incident. 'It's quite a good idea to get to know that procedure—you never know when you might need to perform it!'

'You were marvellous!' cried Archie's wife. 'It all seemed to happen so quickly.' She took out a handkerchief and dabbed her eyes, then laughed shakily. 'I'd certainly want you by me in an emergency, Callum!'

Archie's wife was right, thought Lucy. Callum had reacted incredibly quickly, but with a calm confidence that gave assurance to each person in the room. Not everyone had that unflurried manner when dealing with a crisis, however competent they were. She smiled wryly to herself. She'd be mad not to give him a try in the practice. After all, she'd just had a practical demonstration of his skills!

People were getting up to leave. The shocking incident of Archie's choking fit seemed to have brought the evening to a close, as if the guests hadn't the inclination to be jolly any more. Callum turned towards Lucy and held out his hand.

'Nice to meet you,' he said. 'Let me know soon if there's a chance of a job before I start looking for something else.'

He smiled down at her and Lucy nodded her head decisively. 'I've made up my mind already—bringing Archie back to the land of the living was very impressive so you've certainly passed the practical! If you'd like to have a trial period, I'll offer you the job.'

A broad smile crossed his face. 'Then I'll say thank you, and when can I start?'

'As soon as you like. Come up in a day or so and see the layout. There's a flat at the back of the surgery—it's only tiny, but if you're on your own it might do until you've decided if you like the job.'

'I'll be on my own,' Callum assured her. 'No encumbrances to bother me, and I'm not planning to have any!'

And that, thought Lucy drily, made him sound as uninterested in settling down as she was! She watched him walk out of the room, tall and rangy, his casual clothes sitting well on his broad frame. He seemed to be everything she was looking for in a colleague—why, then, did she have a little niggle of doubt about taking him on? He stopped at the door and looked back, raising his hand in casual farewell, and she felt her pulse give that unaccustomed bound as he looked at her.

'I'll be in touch,' he said. He gave a sudden impish grin. 'And I'll try to measure up to your high standards of efficiency!'

'I'm sure you will,' she murmured, reflecting that the evening certainly hadn't been quite as boring as she'd envisaged!

Callum slid into the back seat of his brother's car and looked back at Lucy's figure silhouetted against the open doorway. He cursed his impetuosity—when he'd had a drink he tended to leap in with both feet. Was he mad to join a practice in the north of Scotland when he hadn't given himself a chance to look at all the options? He hoped he wouldn't regret it, but somehow the offer to take up the job had just slipped out. He had to admit that he liked the idea of working with Lucy—she had the sparky personality of someone who spoke their own mind, and who wasn't interested in flirting. She seemed honest, the sort of girl you could trust to tell the truth, and he valued that now. All the same, staying in London and taking a hospital job where one didn't have time to think might have been more effective in blanking out the memories he was trying so hard to forget—a quiet little place like Ballachter might give too much time for reflection whatever Lucy said about the workload up there.

'You're very quiet, Callum,' said Paul, as they went into the house. 'Anything bothering you?'

Callum grinned ruefully. 'You'll probably think I'm a bit of a fool,' he said, 'but I've just taken a job with Lucy Cunningham's practice in Scotland!'

Paul looked at him in surprise. 'I thought you were going to wait a few weeks before looking for something.'

'I was,' said Callum. 'I hope I've done the right thing!'

CHAPTER TWO

LUCY stopped the car and took several deep breaths of the fresh, astringent Highland air as she got out. How good it had been to get back home from London and in charge of her own life again! She looked lovingly over the wide sweep of fields, a patchwork of gold and green stretching down to the blue of the sea beyond, and to the side of her the small cottage on the hillside where she was going to visit one of her elderly patients. Curlews flew overhead, making their distinctive cry, and the sky was clear and blue—it was like being set free again after being swamped by the noise and crowds of London.

Life had been frantic since she'd returned—Robert Cassidy had been laid low again with another bout of the rheumatoid arthritis that affected him so badly, and she was trying to cover for them both. Thank God she'd got someone to help out at last—Callum was coming the next day, although she still hadn't had a chance to get the flat ready for him.

Lucy felt a nervous frisson of uncertainty flicker through her when she thought about her offer of a job to a man she'd only met briefly over a dinner table. It had all been done so quickly and impulsively—with hindsight perhaps she should have taken more time to make up her mind, but Callum had such an engaging personality and persuasive manner that she suspected she'd allowed her normal caution to fly to the wind—helped by Max's fine wine!

A picture of startling blue eyes flecked with green and twinkling with humour floated into her mind and made her heart jump slightly with excitement and a certain apprehension—an excitement probably engendered purely by relief at having someone else to take the load off her back. She took her medical bag from the front seat of the car and started slowly up the little path to Mrs Souter's cottage. She shrugged. No good worrying now about whether Callum would fit in— they'd just have to rub along together for at least three months!

Mrs Souter shouted at her to come in, and looked up at Lucy from her chair with a relieved smile. 'Hello, Doctor. I was a little worried you might not make it because I know how busy you are, doing most of the work yourself. I did put the kettle on, however, just in case.'

Lucy sat down beside her and looked round appreciatively at the little room, sparkling with cleanliness, although slightly gloomy from the number of pot plants that were Mrs Souter's pride and joy, shielding the light on the window-ledge.

'I won't be doing all the work for much longer, Mrs Souter,' she commented, taking out her stethoscope and warming it for a second on her hand. 'We've got someone coming up to help at last—he's a doctor who's been working in Australia.'

'I hope he knows what he's doing, then! These Aussies live on the other side of the world—they're probably miles behind the times,' observed Mrs Souter illogically.

Lucy grinned and hooked the earpieces into her ears, listening carefully to the old lady's chest. 'I don't think that will make him any less competent.

He's been one of these flying doctors and they have to deal with everything—he probably knows more than I do! Now, take deep breaths in and out so that I can hear the funny noises your lungs have been making.'

The old lady did as she was told, then asked curiously, 'And where will he be staying, then? In that little flat at the back of the surgery?'

Lucy nodded. 'It should be fine for him—he has no family.'

Mrs Souter pursed her lips. 'It's a poky little place—when I was the cleaner at the surgery I used to think you couldn't swing a cat in it!'

'Well, he'll just have to put up with it,' sighed Lucy. 'He seems keen enough to come and says he loves the country, so I hope it lives up to his expectations.'

'I'm sure it will, my dear, with you to show him round. It's a long time since we've had a bachelor doctor!'

For some reason Lucy felt her cheeks colour slightly. Mrs Souter's voice was full of meaning— like most of the elderly ladies round here who kept a motherly eye on their young female doctor, nothing would please them more than that she found someone to settle down with! She delved into her bag and took out her blood-pressure apparatus, then wound the cuff round her patient's arm.

'Let's see if the pressure's lower than last time,' she said briskly. She eyed Mrs Souter with mock sternness. 'I don't think Dr Tate regards himself as a bachelor—he's been married once and has no intention of doing so again. At least, that's my impression!'

Mrs Souter smiled rather knowingly. 'That's what they all say. Given the right circumstances and a very pretty lass, most of them succumb!'

Lucy watched the mercury rise and fall on the sphygmomanometer's dial and said lightly, 'Well, he's just here to do a job of work as far as I'm concerned. As long as he's a good doctor and suits our patients that's all that matters, isn't it?'

'Of course,' murmured Mrs Souter.

Lucy wound the tube round the sphygmomanometer and pushed it back in her bag, changing the subject back firmly to the elderly lady's health. 'Your chest sounds a lot better. Now you've finished your antibiotics, all I want you to stay with is the blood-pressure tablets—they're keeping it down quite well.'

She got up to go, and Mrs Souter pulled herself rather laboriously out of her chair.

'You'll stay and have a cup of tea and a piece of shortbread, will you, my dear?'

Lucy hesitated. She still had to whisk round that darned flat before Callum came, but she was aware that, like so many of her elderly patients who lived in remote areas, Mrs Souter relished company. She smiled at the old lady—it would only take a few minutes of her time.

'That's very kind, Mrs Souter—just a quick cup.'

When she eventually got up to leave, having heard all about Mrs Souter's grandson and how well he was doing at school despite her daughter-in-law being so hopelessly disorganised, Mrs Souter touched Lucy's arm and smiled beguilingly up at her.

'I'll be looking forward to seeing this new young man you've got to help you now, Dr Cunningham.' Her eyes twinkled. 'It'll do you good to have help and a bit of companionship, especially when he can devote all his attention to the practice, having no family himself! With Dr Cassidy being so poorly, you must have been lonely at times.' The old lady sighed. 'And I know what it is to be lonely myself, you know. Sometimes I think I ought to get a little pet to keep me company.'

'You know, that would be a great idea, Mrs Souter. What about a little cat?'

Mrs Souter shook her head gloomily. 'I'm allergic to cats—it would have to be a wee dog.' Then she brightened up. 'You know, I'm really looking forward to meeting this young doctor of yours very soon!'

As Lucy drove away she reflected wryly that soon the whole area would be aware that the new doctor was unattached and therefore most suitable for their young female GP! How much less complicated it would have been if the man had been married with a brood of children. She didn't relish the whole of Ballachter and the surrounding population watching closely for any signs of romance between her and Callum Tate!

Irritably she changed gear forcefully as she descended the steep hill from the moors and into the little town. One of the good things about working up here had been the total lack of any possibility of romance. Nobody around here knew about her past life—she had chosen this remote area to work in for that very reason. She'd needed to make a fresh start three years ago and it had worked out well—young eligible males were very thin on the ground here, and that was how Lucy Cunningham liked it! Never again would she allow herself to fall for a drop-dead gorgeous man who could charm the birds off the trees and fool her into thinking she was the only one for him.

She turned into the small car park of The Lindens, the name by which the surgery was known. It had once been an old family house and was built of the granite of the area and situated at the top of the main village road, just before the fields. It had a homely look, surrounded by a small garden with two small flower-beds filled with lobelias and busy lizzies, which Lucy had planted in the early summer. Since she'd joined the practice three years ago she'd tried to make the place look less clinical, and had added touches like the flowers outside and a children's corner at one end of the large waiting room. Now she was proud of the way it looked—surely anyone joining the practice would be pleasantly surprised.

She squeezed her car with difficulty into the space marked FOR DOCTORS ONLY as a large motorbike parked at an awkward angle had its handlebars protruding over her space. With some irritation she slammed her door closed—there was plenty of room for the bike in the rest of the car park, but it seemed that however many notices were put up, declaring that the spaces were only for the medical staff, patients took no notice.

She flicked a glance at her watch and was pleased to see that she should have plenty of time after all to go through the blood-test results that had been faxed through and sign her repeat prescriptions, then she would do some basic shopping to stock the little flat ready for Callum's arrival the next day. She would ask him round to have a meal with her tomorrow evening and they could discuss the working of the practice then. She was quite relieved that things seemed to be fitting in well and she did want the man to be impressed with the place and to feel he'd come to a practice that was well run.

Lucy pushed the door to the waiting room open and smiled at Bunty, the practice receptionist, who was on the phone, and in her usual brisk way booking in a hospital visit for a patient. Bunty was highly efficient and the practice was her life. Sometimes her efficiency bordered on bossiness, and she could be sharp with patients she thought were wasting her adored doctors' time, but she was totally discreet and reliable. Lucy sometimes thought the whole place would collapse without her stolid presence.

Bunty mouthed something at Lucy and pointed a finger towards Robert Cassidy's consulting room, her facial expression one of excitement mixed with importance. Lucy looked at her enquiringly, wondering whether Robert was feeling slightly better and had come back for the afternoon, then the door of the room opened and, instead of Robert's small frail figure, a large man dressed in biking leathers strode out.

He was tall, with floppy auburn hair, piercing blue eyes and a wide smile, and it took Lucy a few bewildered moments to realise that it was Callum Tate. Her jaw dropped in surprise and she took a deep breath—he looked even more arresting in his biking attire than she remembered from the dinner party! She'd forgotten just how attractive the man was and felt a shiver of surprise at the effect he had on her. Strange how her cardiac rate increased and her stomach somersaulted as if she'd been on a switchback.

A confused babble of thoughts raced round her head. She was taken aback that he'd arrived already—

why hadn't she been more organised and done his flat yesterday, why hadn't she washed her hair like she'd meant to that morning, and just what was Callum doing in Robert's consulting room?

'What on earth are you doing here so soon?' she squeaked. 'I wasn't expecting you till tomorrow—nothing's ready for you yet! I've still got to see to a few things…'

Callum raised a quizzical eyebrow. 'Shall I go back, then? I don't want to be a nuisance!'

Lucy pulled herself together, conscious that this wasn't quite the welcome one should give a new colleague. 'No, no…it's just that you're earlier than I thought you'd be. You see, I've got loads of paperwork to do yet…and the flat's not quite ready either.' She grimaced. It wasn't ready *at all*!

His eyes danced at her and again she experienced the funny flutter of her heart she'd felt a moment ago. 'Sorry to give you such a shock, but I was getting rather bored so I decided I may as well come up today. I thought I could get stuck into work then tomorrow morning.' He gave a wry chuckle. 'Actually, I've been able to start work earlier than that. There's a patient in surgery now, and I hope you don't mind, but I thought in view of his anxiety I'd have a look at him in case you were late back.'

Bunty opened the glass partition of Reception. 'I did try to get you on your mobile, Lucy, but obviously the signal didn't get through and I didn't know how long you'd be.' She looked admiringly up at Callum. 'Dr Tate arrived just as Mr Crawfield came in. Mr Crawfield was in a real panic and demanded to see someone immediately—as usual.' She gave a faint sniff, indicative of her impatience with Mr Crawford, who had a reputation for fussiness, although she was always scrupulous to treat all requests to see the doctor seriously.

Mr Crawfield was the headmaster of the local school, and a frequent visitor to the surgery. Sometimes Lucy thought it was a way of unloading the stress of his job to come and have a really good chat about his health.

'Looks like you've been thrown in at the deep end, then.' She smiled.

'I came out to get a sphygmomanometer,' Callum said. 'I'd like to check his blood pressure—and perhaps you'd like to come and see him, too. I'm sure he'd appreciate his usual doctor being in attendance. He's got pains in his chest—sharp rather than a dull continuous ache, and naturally he's a little het up about it.'

'I can imagine he is, and, of course, I'll come—he's never presented with any sign of heart trouble before, but he seems to find his job very stressful.'

Lucy accompanied him into the room, appreciative of Callum's sensitivity to a patient's nervousness and aware Mr Crawfield might be more relaxed with a doctor he knew.

Mr Crawfield was lying back on the examining table and looked round at the two doctors as they came in, his face tense and deep lines of anxiety etched round his eyes.

'Sorry to trouble you both,' he mumbled. 'It's been a worrying day. I've been in such pain, and even though we're in the middle of exams at the moment, I thought I ought to come and get checked out.'

'You're quite right, Mr Crawfield,' said Lucy soothingly. 'What exactly has been the problem?'

Callum elaborated on what he'd previously told Lucy. 'Mr Crawfield's been experiencing sharp chest pains for some time today, and he's shown me an area in his upper chest that's giving him discomfort.' He inflated the cuff round the man's arm, adding reassuringly, 'That, of course, is a good sign—pain caused by the heart is usually a dull, heavy and continuous ache.'

The man nodded, slightly comforted by this information, then looked nervously at the cuff as it squeezed his arm. 'That's very tight, Doctor—is it supposed to be that uncomfortable?'

'Don't worry, Mr Crawfield. It's only doing its job showing me what your blood pressure is.' He gazed at the gauge on the instrument and smiled. 'Nothing much wrong there, I'm pleased to say—a hundred and twenty over seventy. Teaching all those teenagers must be good for you!'

Mr Crawfield looked astonished. 'My blood pressure's OK, is it?' He shook his head doubtfully. 'But my chest feels so painful when I move—I was sure it must be something to do with my heart.'

Callum put his stethoscope to the man's chest and listened carefully, then looked at the margins of his patient's eyes for signs of anaemia. 'What do you think, Dr Cunningham? Perhaps you'd give a second opinion.'

Lucy also listened to the man's heart and tapped his chest wall for signs of dullness. 'I quite agree with Dr Tate,' she said firmly. 'Your heart sounds absolutely fine—no worries there.'

'Then what can it be? I'm not making this up, you know!' His eyes had a hint of desperation in them as if he felt he was failing to convince the doctors just how bad he felt.

Callum put his hand reassuringly on the man's arm. 'I know you're not making it up, and I'm sure I know what it is…not quite sure what has caused it, though. The clue is that you say it hurts when you move. I want you to stand up and put your arms above your head.'

The man winced as he did so, and Callum put his fingers a little higher on his chest than the patient had indicated the pain had been. 'Still feel it there?' he asked.

'I certainly I do…just as bad. It's stopped now I'm still.'

Callum's eyes met Lucy's and he gave a satisfied little nod. 'I don't think there's any doubt about it, is there, Doctor? I think, Mr Crawfield, that you've strained your chest muscles in the last few days— done something you've forgotten about, no doubt. But that's what it is. If the pain had been something to do with your heart the discomfort would have stayed in the same place no matter what you did with your arms. Moving them moved the strained muscles upwards and the pain leapt up with them. When you keep completely still, the discomfort stops. The pain isn't inside the chest wall—it's on the outside.'

'Really?' Mr Crawfield's anxious-looking face relaxed slightly and then an expression of enlightenment lit his eyes. 'I did do something really strenuous yesterday morning, actually—I'd forgotten all about it—lifting a lot of tables from the school dining room to the gym. The caretaker's off at the moment and we're having a parents' supper at the end of the week…' He looked in an embarrassed way at the two doctors, both of them smiling at his relief. 'You'll think I'm a fool,' he murmured.

'Of course not,' said Callum firmly. 'Any chest pain should be investigated. Luckily your discomfort will wear off in a few days—and you can enjoy the parents' supper!'

Lucy watched Mr Crawfield almost bounce his way out of the room, his face looking years younger in his relief. She smiled to herself. She felt a huge surge of relief, too. Having watched Callum in action and how he dealt with the anxious patient, she was sure she had not made a mistake in offering him the job.

'You've made one worried headmaster very happy,' she remarked. 'I'm glad you came a day early!'

Callum followed her out to the little kitchen at the back of Reception where Bunty was making tea and filling a large plate with biscuits.

'That looks good,' murmured Callum. 'Biking up here from London sure makes you thirsty.'

'Don't you have a car?' asked Bunty curiously. 'It's going to get rather cold in the winter when you do visits, isn't it?'

'I might get one eventually,' he said. 'At the moment I can get everywhere very quickly—even bypass flocks of sheep or cows moving on the road.' He bestowed one of his devastating smiles at Bunty whose round little face blushed furiously. 'We've had rather a cursory introduction already…I guess you're the driving force in the practice!'

'You're right,' said Lucy, amused at Bunty's reaction to his flattery. 'Bunty Heron keeps the whole place running smoothly—she's a treasure!' She turned to Callum. 'I'll take you to the flat now—it's really only the bed that needs making up, and then we can go to the shops and stock up.'

'I can do all that myself,' Callum said, smiling. 'Just show me the way.'

Bunty handed Lucy the key of the flat and looked up appreciatively at Callum's tall figure, which seemed to dominate the small room. 'I hope you'll enjoy it here, Dr Tate. It'll be good for Lucy to have some help. She's run off her feet at the moment—and none of the patients seem to appreciate that.'

He laughed. 'That's the trouble with patients— they're a real nuisance, always being ill and bothering the doctors! And by the way, my name's Callum. I may be the doctor to the patients, but I hope we'll regard each other as colleagues.'

Lucy led the way through the back of the surgery to the little extension which had been built onto the original building at one time as accommodation for an elderly relative. Honeysuckle and roses had softened the aspect of the newer stone and from the outside it looked pretty. She opened the door and a rather musty damp smell drifted out. Guiltily she wondered how long it was since the windows had been opened.

'I think you'll like it, although it is quite small...' She paused for a moment and then gave a sharp intake of breath. 'Oh, heavens!' she whispered, her eyes glued to the step.

A small gush of water dribbled through the open door from the hallway and trickled slowly down the path. She followed its progress with mesmerised eyes.

'Look what's happened!' She clutched Callum's arm in horror. 'I don't believe this! The whole thing's under water!'

Callum pushed forward and peered in through the

door. 'Let me go in and see—it may be nothing much. Probably looks worse than it is...'

'You can't go in now—you'll get soaked.'

'Don't worry, my boots are pretty waterproof.' Gently he disengaged his arm from her convulsive clutch and pushed past her, sloshing through the water in the little hallway. She heard him give a low whistle. 'Looks like a tank's leaking in the roof—there's rather a lot of water coming through the ceiling. Where's the stop tap? I'll turn it off.'

Stop tap? Practical things like that rarely entered Lucy's head, and again she had a horrible vision of herself boasting to Callum at the dinner party about her wonderful organisational abilities. What a fool she looked like now! She tore off her shoes and waded in behind him, grimacing. 'I'm not quite sure.... Perhaps it's under the sink or in the bathroom.'

She looked incredulously round the small flat. It looked rather like a scene from the *Titanic*, a soap dish floating incongruously past her from the bathroom, tables and chairs in the little kitchen looking forlorn in their ponds of water.

Callum paddled over to the sink and peered under the cupboard. 'Ah, you're right! Here it is. I'll turn it off here, and then we'll turn on all the taps and empty the tank so that at least it won't keep on flooding.'

'I'm terribly sorry,' Lucy said mournfully. 'What a welcome! I'm not quite as efficient as I told you, am I?'

He laughed. 'I took it you referred to work, not domestic issues. Anyway, I should think you've had other things to worry about in the last few days. I hear your partner, Robert Cassidy, isn't very well and everything's devolved on you?'

Lucy captured the floating soap dish and placed it on a window-ledge. 'That's right,' she sighed. 'Actually, I'm relieved you've come early—if we can find you a place to stay!'

'That shouldn't be difficult, surely. There's loads of bed and breakfasts about, aren't there? To cater for people who come for the fishing and golf?'

'I bet there isn't a space in the town at the moment. There's a huge country show, coupled with the Highland Games, coming soon, and over the next few weeks there's a film crew here, making an epic about the Highland clearances in the eighteenth century.'

'Looks like I'll have to kip in the storeroom of the surgery, then,' Callum said lightly. 'Sounds as if Ballachter is a hive of activity and not the little backwater your mother suggested!'

'She's never been here,' said Lucy shortly. 'She has absolutely no idea what it's like—she just thinks it's a place where one gets forgotten and where I have no chance of meeting Mr Right!'

He looked at her quizzically, his gaze sweeping over her slightly flushed cheeks and the large dark eyes flashing with indignation. 'And have you met Mr Right?'

Lucy didn't know why her reply came out so vehemently or defensively. 'No, I have not...which is not to say I don't have a very good social life. '

'I'm sure you do...' He turned away, starting to turn the taps on in the sink. 'I suspect your mother would like to run your life,' he murmured.

'Too right she would! I'm afraid I'm not like my sister, who's managed to fulfill all my mother's ambitions for her.' Lucy bit her lip. She was beginning to sound bitter, and she didn't feel that way—not any more. She made an effort to turn the subject and sound more upbeat. 'Look here—I've plenty of room in my house. You're very welcome to stay if you don't mind a rather supercilious cat that seems to have adopted me!'

'You sure about that? I don't want to put you out…'

'Quite sure!' declared Lucy emphatically. 'Come on, let's get out of here. I'll ring the plumber now and try and get someone to come urgently.'

'That's very kind of you. I'll be the perfect guest!'

His eyes twinkled down at her, and suddenly Lucy wondered if she'd done the right thing. When he looked at her like that her stomach seemed to revolve like the drum in a washing-machine. Callum Tate was just a bit too darned attractive, and at the moment he was standing so very close to her. It had been a long time since any man had had this startling effect on her—almost as if he'd activated an electric current that had been dormant for some time, and had sent it rippling alarmingly through her body. The feeling was unfamiliar and…well, just a bit scary! She moved towards the door away from him, her feet making little splashing sounds as she waded along.

'We'll go there now if you like,' she said from the safety of the front door. 'You can take off your wet things and have a shower then.'

Her easy assurances that she had plenty of room had not been quite accurate—it was just a terrace cottage with a minute kitchen and one very small living room. It was going to seem even smaller with a large man like Callum installed there!

'You're sure you'll be all right on this bed?' asked Lucy, looking rather doubtfully at the small single bed squashed in between her desk and a bookcase. The room doubled as a guest room and her office, and suddenly it seemed absolutely minute!

'Of course I will—it's the height of luxury compared to some places I've spent the night, although there's more space when you sleep beneath the stars in the Australian bush and see them wheeling above you in a velvety sky.' He smiled at her. 'You'd love it—there's nothing like falling asleep under the stars.'

A quick vision of herself lying alone next to Callum in the vastness of the Australian outback swam into Lucy's imagination and sent little goose-bumps jumping up her arms.

She spoke rather breathlessly. 'It must be very beautiful. I've often thought I'd like to visit Australia. Won't you miss it all terribly?'

She wondered if he missed anything else—his ex-wife, for instance? Or was he really over her and ready to start a new life here?

Callum bent down and looked through the small window at the side of the bed and gave a low whistle. 'This beautiful view is just as breathtaking as anything in Australia—I shall enjoy waking up to that! You look as though you've your own private loch.'

'That's just a little inlet from the sea, and the huge field to the side of it is where they have the country show. I'm on duty at the show and Highland Games—there's plenty of opportunity for injury.'

'I look forward to that—I've always wanted to see the caber being tossed!'

She laughed up at him, her cheeks dimpling. 'There's more to the games than that, you know!'

The low sun of evening streamed through the window and caught the sheen of her silky hair, and her eyes looked large in the dying light. For a second Callum looked at her strangely, then he put his hand out and gently touched her arm.

'Looks like there's going to be plenty to enjoy here,' he murmured. 'I think we'll work well together.'

CHAPTER THREE

LUCY couldn't sleep, tossing restlessly around in her bed until the bedclothes were rumpled and she was more wide awake than in the middle of the day. The weather had deteriorated—she could hear the wind howling against the little house and the rain battering the windows—but that wasn't what was keeping her awake. She just couldn't seem to obliterate her thoughts of Callum lying only a few yards away on the other side of the wall in the little spare room— the man seemed to have taken a frightening grip on her mind. Images of him floated round and round in her head and every nerve end in her body seemed to prickle in response to his irresistible attraction when they were together.

She'd become like a teenager, she told herself scornfully, taken completely unawares and allowing Callum to push everything normal out of her head. How could she work professionally with someone she thought about in that way, even though she'd only known him for a few hours?

Was it going to be like this for the next few days until the flat was ready, her skipping out of his way when they went to bed? She'd already had a disturbing sight of him coming out of the bathroom clad only in a towel wrapped round his waist and revealing a tanned broad chest. She'd retreated hastily to her own room until she'd been quite sure he'd disappeared!

She gave a little shiver and cuddled further under

the bedclothes, trying to banish the man from her consciousness. But it was no good. His looks, his voice, his whole manner seemed to dominate her, and it was frightening—frightening because it was so sudden, so unexpected. A few days ago she'd been coasting along quite happily, secure in the knowledge that her life was her own. She'd been in control of what she did and no one had been able to manipulate her, bend her to their will.

Finally, in despair at ever getting off to sleep, she sat bolt upright in bed and decided to make herself a hot cup of tea and read the latest medical journal for a while. Surely that would get the man out of her mind!

To her surprise the light was on in the kitchen and a deep voice was saying, 'Just a small bowl of milk, then, puss, and that's your lot!'

Lucy pushed open the door and Callum looked round at her, his hair untidily rumpled round his head and the towel still just about clinging round his waist. Daisy, her little cat, was entwining herself round his legs and purring contentedly. Even the cat could see his attractions!

'Couldn't you sleep either?' he asked with a quizzical grin. 'Let me make you my special nightcap developed for insomnia—hot cocoa with a little shot of Australian whisky. Never fails!'

'Sure,' she said faintly, wondering what it was that had kept him awake as well. She wished she'd put on a dressing-gown to hide her very serviceable flannel stripy pyjamas, and she wished she'd stayed in her room. Suddenly the little kitchen seemed terribly small and intimate with the two of them in it. She was only too aware of just what a strapping physique

Callum had and, however used she was to seeing male torsos in a medical setting, somehow being only a foot or two from that gorgeous masculine chest was having a distinctly non-medical effect on her. It was amazing how loud her thudding heart seemed to be!

'I...I thought I'd come down and get the latest medical journal—there's rather an interesting article on the treatment of diabetics in it.'

'Good night-time reading, eh? It would certainly get me off to sleep!'

Lucy giggled nervously. Perhaps she had sounded a little sanctimonious. 'You're probably right—the cocoa will be much more enjoyable!'

She sipped from the steaming cup cautiously, letting the hot comforting liquid slip down her throat, gently relaxing her. Callum leant his long frame against the fridge and looked at her thoughtfully.

'So, you've made a real life for yourself up here, it seems. No regrets about leaving your family in London—no ties to keep you down there?'

'Not at all. I love my sister very dearly, but I need to plough my own furrow away from them all.'

'And you've no other brothers or sisters?'

Lucy put the cup down very carefully on the worktop and brushed a crumb rather fastidiously from her pyjamas. Her voice had an unusual hardness. 'I have a stepsister, Gina. My mother's been married twice, and Gina is her daughter by her first husband who died when they were quite young.'

'And is your father still alive?'

Lucy shrugged and stared out through the window into the black night. 'He might as well be dead. He left my mother when I was about seven. I remember

him very well because I adored him, and I don't think
I've ever got over him walking out on us.'

There was a second's silence, then Callum took a
pace towards her and put his hands on her shoulders,
looking down very kindly into her eyes. 'That's a
terrible thing to happen to a child,' he said softly. 'It
must have torn you apart...'

'It did—and I can never forgive him.'

'Then you know all about a child's hopes and fears
in the same situation,' he said gently.

Lucy looked away to prevent him seeing the bright
tears that still welled up in her eyes when she thought
about her father's betrayal. She was acutely aware of
Callum's comforting strong hands on her shoulders
and the warm sympathy in those blue eyes. How
tempting, how easy it would be to lean her head on
his shoulder and tell him everything that had happened to her—the whole sad story that had forced her
to move away from London. Then she bit her lip and
slipped away from him, picking up her cup and sipping the hot liquid.

She must stop thinking about Callum in this way,
she told herself angrily. She'd only known the man
for such a short time—one evening, to be precise! It
was extraordinary that after so short an acquaintance
she should be unburdening herself to him, telling him
things she hesitated to discuss with her best friend.

'I know what effect divorce had on me, my mother
and my sister,' she said simply. 'But up here I feel I
can put that behind me.'

'I'm sure you can,' said Callum softly.

The silence that fell between them was harshly broken by the strident ringing of the phone. Lucy shot a
look at the clock on the little dresser. 'I didn't tell

you I'm on call tonight,' she said ruefully. 'We have an arrangement with the two nearest practices to take it in turns from l0 p.m. to 7 a.m. Looks like I'm going to be on duty after all.'

She picked up the phone. 'Dr Cunningham here— how can I help?'

Callum watched her as she talked to the caller, her heart-shaped face serious, the delicately arched brows frowning slightly. She was startlingly attractive, but totally unaware of it, and there was a vulnerability about her that perhaps came from her past and made her so different from her confident sister. He smiled wryly to himself. Most of the beautiful girls he'd come across were only too conscious of their desirability and, as he knew to his cost, used it to get what they wanted. Lucy Cunningham, he reflected suddenly, would not deceive—she would tell things as they were. Honesty and desirability—now, that was a very powerful attraction, he reflected thoughtfully. It was a funny thing, but a few days ago he'd thought he'd never trust or be attracted to another woman again, but suddenly…

Lucy put down the phone. 'Have to go. One of my expectant mums has gone into labour at a farm about three miles up the road and the midwife's car has broken down in the middle of nowhere. Sounds as if everything's taking off rather quickly so I'd better go before the baby arrives on its own.'

'Then let me come as well. I'd like to get to know your patients. If she doesn't want to see me, I can keep the father talking!'

'It might take ages. One of us should get some sleep!'

He smiled. 'You look pretty tired to me. Doing the

work of two people must be exhausting. Wouldn't you like some back-up?'

It was a very tempting offer. Lucy did feel exhausted—probably a mixture of hard work and emotional turmoil—and it was a horrible night.

'If you're sure. It is a bit lonely, going along those country roads at two o'clock in the morning, but it would be a help! We'd better go and put something more suitable on!'

It was pitch dark as Lucy drove down the narrow country lane and the rain had not abated—a lashing cloudburst was hitting the windscreen so hard the wipers could hardly cope. She flicked a covert glance at Callum by her side, and felt a rush of thankfulness that he'd suggested coming. It would have been quite frightening, driving alone in these conditions.

'Bill and Kath Forsyth are lovely people,' she shouted above the noise of the rain and the car engine. 'The sheep farm's been in their family for generations. They've been married for five years and I think they were beginning to lose hope of having a baby. They'd just started to ask about IVF treatment when she found out she was pregnant!'

'And was she booked in for a home birth?'

'Yes. She was adamant that, unless there was a very good reason to the contrary, she would have the baby at the farm. She's about three weeks early and she can't have envisaged the midwife getting stuck on such a lousy night. From the sound of it, the baby's making quick progress!'

Callum chuckled. 'This reminds me of going to some of the remote homesteads in the bush. Babies seem to prefer coming at the most awkward time of night!'

Lucy peered through the drenched windscreen and slowed down as a light appeared at the end of a lane she was going to turn into. A desperate-looking face, dripping with rain, thrust itself towards the window as Lucy stopped.

'Thank God, someone's here at last. I thought we'd been abandoned!' The man was gabbling, his voice on the edge of panic. 'For pity's sake, step on it, please. Kath's not got long to go now, I can tell...'

'Get in the back, Bill,' shouted Lucy. 'Is anyone with her?'

'My mother's there,' panted Bill as he climbed into the car. 'She's very frail, though, and I don't know if she can do much...'

'You've delivered enough animals in your time—can't you tell if things are going well?'

The agitated man gave a groan. 'It's not the same, Doctor. I know what I'm doing with the animals. It's different with your own wife! Kath's in such pain, and I can't help her. What if the cord's round the baby's neck? Suppose she has a protracted labour and the baby gets distressed? And it's coming early—that could mean it's a very low birth weight...'

Lucy laughed. 'Calm down, Bill, your imagination's working overtime! You're thinking of the worst-case scenarios. The baby is a little early, it's true, but it may have gained respectable weight anyway. Now, this is my new colleague, Dr Callum Tate. Perhaps when we get there you could put some tea on together while I go upstairs and see Kath. Try not to worry—Kath's had a marvellous pregnancy.'

Once in the house, Callum took Bill by the arm.

'Let's do the time-honoured thing, Mr Forsyth,' he said firmly, 'and put on plenty of hot water. Lead me to the kitchen!'

Lucy made her way upstairs and into the large rather gloomy bedroom where Kath was lying on the bed and her mother-in-law was sponging her forehead with a damp cloth. They were chatting quietly to each other and both looked totally calm and in control. Lucy almost laughed.

'I thought I'd find hysterics,' she remarked. 'Bill indicated that it was bedlam up here.'

Kath shook her head hopelessly. 'That man's lost all sense. He's delivered hundreds of animals in his life, but one baby coming along and you'd think it was the end of the world! He's been rushing round like someone demented! Nevertheless, we are glad to see you, aren't we, Nan?'

'We certainly are,' said the old lady. 'It was a bit worrying when we heard the midwife was stranded. It's been a long time since I had my children and I don't know that I can remember what to do! Now I can go and get the clean towels and sheets you'll probably be wanting, Doctor.'

Lucy started to take instruments out of her bag. 'That's good of you. If we'd known the baby would be born three weeks early the midwife would have left packs of towelling to be used—but the ones you get will be just as good.' She smiled down at Kath, who was beginning to screw her face up and clench her fist as a contraction started. 'You're doing great there, Kath. Have you timed them yet?'

The girl's features relaxed as the contraction ended and she took a deep breath. 'About every five minutes now. My waters broke earlier this evening and it all seemed to progress very quickly. I just didn't have time to get nervous. Mary Maclachlan, the midwife, said she could be with me in half an hour. Turns out she couldn't make it after all...'

'Well, it looks like you've been doing excellently by yourself. Let's have a listen to the little one's heart and see how he or she's coping.'

Lucy took the small foetal Doppler out of her bag and smeared some lubricating jelly on Kath's abdomen, then ran the small machine over the bump. Into the quiet of the room came the pattering sound of the little heart, regular and strong. The two women's eyes met in delight and a large smile spread over Kath's face.

'Wow!' she whispered. 'It sounds good!'

'It's a wonderful noise, isn't it?' said Lucy. The beat began to sound slightly more rapid. 'I guess another contraction's coming up now—try and relax, Kath. Breathe in and out, in and out. I think another few moments and we'll see this baby begin to show.'

Kath gripped Lucy's hand, then as the contraction died down struggled to sit up.

'Where's Bill?' she asked. 'It would be just like him to miss the flaming birth. He was actually late for his own wedding!'

Callum stood at the door. 'I don't want to intrude,' he said, 'but could you do with any help?'

'Kath,' said Lucy, 'this is Dr Tate—a new colleague of mine. Would you mind if he assisted me now the birth is so near?'

Kath shook her head. 'If he's delivered babies before, he's very welcome to help. But I want Bill here as well.' Her voice was fretful and Lucy patted her hand soothingly.

'We'll get him for you, sweetheart…he's only downstairs.'

'He's actually been boiling kettles like mad—there's enough steam down there to drive Stephenson's Rocket!' remarked Callum.

Kath managed a weak smile as another strong contraction overcame her, then her mother-in-law came back into the room, her small figure bowed under a pile of towels and sheets.

'How's it doing, Doctor?' she asked. 'Any progress yet?'

'Kath would like Bill here,' said Lucy. 'And I think she's right—things are beginning to happen now!'

'Of course I'm right,' gasped Kath, clutching Lucy's hand. 'Suddenly I need to push. I can't stop it—the baby's coming!'

Callum nodded at Lucy. 'I can see the crown of the baby's head now,' he said calmly. 'Your baby has black hair like his dad!'

Lucy spread a large towel under Kath, then she and Callum washed their hands in the bedroom basin and put on latex gloves from sealed packs in Lucy's bag.

'You're doing so well, Kath. Pant a little now, we don't want the baby to shoot out too quickly. When I tell you to push, put your chin on your chest and push for all you're worth!'

'Where's Bill?' Kath's voice was rising slightly. 'He mustn't miss it!' She gripped Lucy's hand convulsively and grunted with effort.

A hoarse voice replied from the door. 'I'm here, love. Don't worry. I'm with you!'

Kath gave a sudden gasp, there was a wet, gushing noise and Lucy bent forward and caught the slippery little body firmly as it slithered into the world after nine months in its cosy sanctuary.

'Welcome to the big wide world, little one,' she said softly, as she swiftly wrapped the baby in a warm blanket, and Callum cut and clamped the umbilical cord. Then very gently she handed the baby to Kath.

'Congratulations, Kath and Bill—you have a beautiful little boy and he looks quite hefty to me!'

The baby let out a lusty cry, and there was a heavy crash in the doorway as Bill fainted dead away.

They left the mother peacefully asleep, exhausted after all her efforts, her little boy cosily wrapped up in a small crib beside her bed. Bill had recovered and was now shakily handing out glasses of champagne to his mother and the two doctors.

'We'll only have a sip to wet the baby's head,' said Lucy. 'We're on duty in a few hours. But it's been a lovely start to the day!'

'Thanks for all your help,' said Bill gruffly. 'And to you, Dr Tate. You kept me busy, and I might not have made it to the room at all without you calming me down—although,' he added shamefacedly, 'I wasn't much help when I got there!'

Callum grinned. 'It's sometimes harder to be the father than the one giving birth, I imagine!' He raised his glass. 'Here's to baby Robert. I certainly won't forget my first night in the practice!'

The dawn was touching the horizon as they drove home. Streaks of pale blue and pink ribboned the sky and the rain and wind had gone.

Callum had offered to drive, and Lucy had gladly accepted. Her car was insured for any colleagues to drive and although she felt the elation and excitement of the past two hours, she knew that soon she would flop.

'What a night,' she murmured, relaxing back in relief. 'I don't know about the mother, but I feel as if I've almost given birth to that baby!'

Callum smiled and glanced across at her. 'It's a pretty good feeling, isn't it, helping a baby into the world? A good birth like that puts me on a high every time!'

'Me, too,' said Lucy. 'She's a lucky woman—a perfect baby to look after!'

'Motherhood appeals to you, then?' Callum murmured. 'Delivering babies hasn't put you off having them?'

'Of course not. To me, children would add an extra dimension—but not yet awhile.' Lucy paused and flicked a glance at his firm profile as he negotiated the twisting road before him. 'And you? Would you like a family?'

He shrugged. 'Sure, that's what I hoped for when I got married.' He was silent for a second then said tersely, 'Unfortunately my wife didn't feel the same. She told me on our honeymoon that children weren't an option, although before our wedding she'd seemed enthusiastic.' He gave a mirthless laugh. 'Turned out marriage to me wasn't really her cup of tea either...'

'Oh, Callum, that's awful...' Lucy's voice trailed away, unable to think of adequate words to say.

From his demeanour one would never have suspected Callum of having been in a disappointing marriage in the past. No wonder he had stated so firmly at the dinner party that he had no encumbrances, and wasn't likely to either! It had probably put him off marriage for life, and she wondered what kind of a woman could treat a man like Callum so cruelly.

She gave a gasp as the car gave a sudden jolt and Callum stamped on the brake so hard that they skidded across the road, screaming to a halt before a huge water-filled hole stretched across the road.

His arm came across Lucy's body to keep her back in her seat, although the seat belts had saved them from hitting the windscreen.

'Hell!' he whispered. 'This must have been caused by the night's rain.'

They sat in shock for a moment, then he remarked, 'Going to be difficult to get round that.'

They both got out of the car and gazed at the road in stunned silence, then Lucy pulled out her mobile phone and rapidly punched in some numbers. 'I'd better let the police know—we can't stay here for ever!'

Callum threw back his head and laughed. 'I can see why you moved up here—the life in London was too quiet, wasn't it? You'll be sending me on a mountain rescue next—it's about the only thing we've not done tonight!'

Lucy grinned. 'Never a dull moment here…'

Someone had answered the phone and she spoke briskly into it, giving the location and nature of the road obstruction.

'They'll take at least fifteen minutes,' she told Callum ruefully as she put the mobile back in her pocket. 'There's been a number of flooded roads and they're at full stretch.'

'It could be worse—at least it's stopped raining. Look at that sun rising in the sky—and the light bathing those fields. It's magnificent, isn't it?'

There was a stillness in the air that came just before

the day started properly, and somewhere in the background a thrush began to sing. Callum smiled down at Lucy, his eyes dancing with humour.

'If we've got to be marooned, I can't think of a more lovely place.'

His hand came up and stroked away a stray lock of hair from her forehead, his glance lingering on her face. For a second their gazes locked, and suddenly his expression changed and the blue in his eyes darkened.

'We worked well together, didn't we?' he said softly.

'Yes. Yes, we did.'

His other hand came up and he held her head gently between his hands. 'It's a funny old world,' he whispered. 'I feel as if I've known you a long time...'

'Only a few hours really...' Lucy's voice was breathless, she could hardly get the words out.

'Enough to know you're a very special person.' He sighed softly. 'And a very beautiful one, too.'

Lucy wanted to shout at him, No you don't—nobody knows what I'm really like. A warning shiver raced through her body. This was happening far too quickly. Those flattering phrases that came off his tongue seemed so glib—surely she was wise enough not to believe them? She stared at Callum, frightened by the extraordinary surge of energy that suddenly crackled like electricity between them and still feeling the exhilaration prompted by the rush of adrenalin which came so often at the end of a dramatic situation.

She was rooted to the spot, caught like a rabbit in headlights, but she managed to croak feebly, 'No... don't say that...'

'Why not? It's true, Lucy…'

Her heart started to slam very hard against her ribs. She knew what was going to happen and it was madness. But he was so very close to her, his breath on her cheek, his hair whipping into hers as he pressed his warm hard body hip to hip against her. She knew as he brushed his firm lips against her mouth that it was too late to pull herself away.

His kiss became more demanding, harder, intrusive, and she closed her eyes, allowing her body to respond as she arched herself against his muscular body. She felt a sob rising in her throat. This felt so wonderful, and it had been so long since anyone had done this to her, or she'd wanted them to. Her head lolled back, and his lips trailed a trace of fire down her neck, his arms wrapped hard around her, supporting her body, and she could feel how much he wanted her. Suddenly Lucy didn't care about restraint any more. She hardly knew this man, but she was sure she wanted him with all her mind and body to make love to her. She parted her lips slightly and felt the sweetness of his mouth, the electric touch of his hands moving over her body.

They didn't hear the car drawing up beyond the hole in the road. It was the gentle hoot of a horn that made them spring apart and look guiltily towards the sound. A policeman got out and grinned at them.

'Sorry to disturb you,' he called out cheerily. 'Thought you'd like to know that the fire engine will be here in a minute to pump out the water and get you across safely—or perhaps,' he added cheekily, 'you'd like me to tell them to take their time!'

Lucy pulled herself away from Callum, not daring to look at him, feeling foolish and dazed. The interruption had brought her back to reality with an embarrassing bump, and all she could think of was that the whole of Ballachter would know about her indiscretion very soon! Her face flamed with chagrin and she turned and got into the car, leaning back for a second against the seat, her eyes closed. What the hell was happening to her? After all her vows that she would never get entangled with a man again, she'd got herself into a compromising position with someone she had to work with—and someone she barely knew! Callum got in beside her and flicked a glance at her stony face.

'Rather rudely interrupted there, I'm afraid,' he said lightly.

Lucy sat up very straight, staring in front of her. 'I'm sorry,' she said abruptly. 'We shouldn't have done that…'

He looked at her perceptively, caught by her stricken tone of voice. 'I thought you enjoyed it,' he said gently.

'That's not the point, is it? We're colleagues— we've got to work together. We can't do this sort of thing. And anyway…' she turned to him, her face white and strained '…you want a relationship and any sort of commitment as little as I do at the moment, so let's leave it at that. It was momentary madness, that's all!'

'If that's the way you want it, Lucy,' he said quietly.

Callum started up the engine as the fire engine arrived and soon he was edging his way slowly over the planks they'd laid across the huge hole. His fingers were tensed tightly round the steering-wheel, and he cursed himself angrily. How could he have lost

control like that—allowed himself to give into the
overwhelming and amazing attraction he found himself feeling towards this woman that he barely knew?
He cursed his impulsive nature that led him to do
things he sometimes regretted. The trouble was, he'd
had no idea that he would feel this way about a
woman ever again after Tamsin, and it had taken him
totally by surprise.

He glanced quickly across at Lucy's expressionless
face. He wanted to work with her, and he didn't want
to spoil things between them before he'd barely
started the job. He gripped the wheel even tighter. It
would be like treading on glass but, whatever happened, he had to find out just why it was that Lucy
was so wary of men.

CHAPTER FOUR

THE waiting room looked very full indeed. Lucy's heart sank as she made her way through crying babies and sneezing and coughing adults. It was summertime, but it seemed the whole population of Ballachter was afflicted with heavy colds!

'Rather a big list for you today, Lucy,' said Bunty cheerfully. 'Could you see a little girl first who's having a screaming fit? Hurt her finger apparently.'

'Of course,' replied Lucy heavily, hoping the aspirin she'd taken for a throbbing headache would take effect soon.

After the night she'd just had—and the awkward way it had ended—what she really needed right now was a quiet day at home and a good sleep. She peered gloomily into the mirror hanging up by the noticeboard and shuddered. Pink eyes in a white face and ragged hair—she looked worse than many of her patients!

'Any coffee going, Bunty?' she asked. 'I could do with a pick-me-up before I tackle the day!'

'Sure—there's some ready now.' Bunty poured her a cup and looked at her sympathetically. 'I believe you had a strenuous night—all kinds of excitement. I spoke to Mary Maclachlan, and she told me you had to deliver Bill and Kath Forsyth's baby when she got stranded. What a night, eh?'

'Er…yes, it certainly was…'

In more ways than one, reflected Lucy, sipping the

hot liquid gratefully. She felt a flush of embarrassment when she thought how she'd reacted to Callum's
kisses. What on earth had made her come on to him
like that, encouraging him to think...what, that she
fancied him like mad? For some reason she'd thrown
good sense out of the window over a man she barely
knew, a man who'd recently been divorced and was
probably leaping easily from one relationship to another. Anyway, the last thing she wanted was to get
involved with someone she worked with. She stared
gloomily ahead of her. Things were bound to be
slightly awkward between them now.

She took a deep breath and pushed her pessimistic
thoughts to the back of her mind—back to reality and
dealing with a frightened child who was roaring her
head off.

'Bethany Layton,' she called from her door.

The little girl was plump, with round wire-rimmed
glasses and a gap in her teeth. She looked very, very
scared and big tears were spilling under the glasses
and down her round cheeks. One hand was clinging
to her mother's, the other was held out by her side.

'It hurts,' she whimpered, then, opening her mouth
wider, she yelled, '*It hurts!*'

'I'm sure it does, Bethany,' Lucy said soothingly,
'and we're going to try and make it better very soon.
Will you let me look at it properly?'

She bent forward to examine her small patient's
finger and caught sight of a staple under Bethany's
finger just before Bethany snatched her hand away
and turned to bury her head in her mother's skirts,
screaming uncontrollably.

Lucy sighed. This wasn't going to be easy. A ter-
rified small child with something caught under her

fingernail was not going to let her do much. She glanced up at the young mother, looking almost as white and stricken as her daughter.

'How did she manage to get the staple under her nail, Mrs Layton?'

'She was playing at her father's desk, and there was a stapler there. She must have seen him staple papers together…'

'So she tried to do the same with her own fingers!' finished Lucy wryly.

She took out a book from her desk drawer which showed lots of pictures of happy children in a surgery being attended to by the doctor.

'Would you just read this to Bethany for a minute, Mrs Layton? I'm going to ask a colleague to help me with this.'

Mrs Layton looked alarmed. 'Oh, dear, what are you going to do?'

'Nothing awful, I promise, but the more quickly we can get it out, the better. And perhaps,' she added rather optimistically, 'Bethany will hardly notice!'

It was a pity the practice nurse was very busy, changing dressings on patients who'd had minor ops, Lucy thought wryly. It looked as if the only option was to ask Callum if he could help. She felt dog-tired and emotionally drained—too much had happened too quickly the night before, and she didn't feel like talking to him yet. She walked through the waiting area, barely registering the people sitting there, feeling instead the sensation of two arms wrapped round her, soft lips covering her neck with kisses and a hard body pressed against hers…

She should have treated the episode as a light-hearted moment. Instead, she'd made a big deal of it, talking about 'commitment' and 'relationships' when it probably hadn't crossed Callum's mind that there was any sort of tie between them at all!

She forced these thoughts to the back of her head and brought herself back to the matter in hand.

'Is Callum with anyone at the moment?' she asked Bunty, who was briskly dealing with two patients who both insisted they were booked in at the same time.

'No, he's just going through the list of visits to be done today and looking at the map to get an idea where everyone lives.' Bunty turned back to one of the women looking belligerently at her through the glass panel and said firmly, 'There appears to have been a misunderstanding, ladies. I think the best thing is to take you in alphabetical order—Mrs Anderson to go first.'

The two patients trotted obediently back to their seats, cowed by Bunty's crisp voice, and Lucy knocked on Callum's door and walked in, trying to look businesslike and detached. He looked up enquiringly, a slight wariness in his eyes when he saw it was Lucy.

'Can I help?'

Her smile was stiff, her voice a little strained. 'I hope so. I've a little girl in my room with a staple stuck under her nail. I think she's going to need a local anaesthetic as she's very agitated, and it's obviously so painful she's never going to allow me to touch it. Could you inject her and then I'll remove it.'

He smiled as if relieved that was all she wanted. 'Fine—I'll bring Herbert with me.'

'Herbert?'

Callum grinned. 'Herbert goes through a great deal in his quest to help children—injections, medicines, eyedrops. He has them every day!'

He took out of the rucksack he seemed to carry with him everywhere a large teddy bear with an endearing smile on its face. 'He's calmed more children and their parents than any sedative could ever do!' he remarked as they went back to Lucy's room.

Bethany had quietened down somewhat and was now sitting on her mother's knee, looking at the book, but on seeing the two doctors her lips started to wobble ominously.

Callum sat down quickly opposite her and held out the bear. 'This is Herbert,' he said, 'and I'm his friend, Dr Tate. He's got a staple stuck in his paw, too, and we're going to give him a magic medicine so that it won't hurt. Could you help me to make him better?'

The child held out her good arm and cuddled the toy while Lucy made a pretence of injecting its arm. Callum used a pair of tweezers in a show of removing a staple. Bethany looked impressed.

'Is he all right now?' she asked, her eyes round with wonder behind the wire glasses.

'He certainly is,' said Callum jovially. 'Now, could you cuddle Herbert while I look at your poorly finger, too? We'll find a little plaster for you to put round Herbert's paw in a minute.'

What a magical touch he had with children, thought Lucy, watching as the child's attention was diverted to looking after the bear—it was hard that his wife hadn't wanted to have children. Callum looked as if he'd make an ideal father. She held Bethany's finger firmly and before the child noticed, Callum injected it with lignocaine. There was an immediate yell from Bethany, but soon the local anaesthetic began to do its work and the finger went numb. While Callum kept the child's attention diverted by a long story about Herbert, Lucy managed to work the staple out from under the nail with a small file.

She looked triumphantly at Mrs Layton. 'There! All done now. We'll wrap up the finger for a while until the anaesthetic's worn off.'

The white-faced mother looked as though she was going to faint. 'I...I don't feel too good,' she whispered. 'I've never been very brave at watching this sort of thing.'

Lucy smiled sympathetically. 'Why don't you sit down for a minute in the waiting room to recover? I'm sure the receptionist will give you a cup of tea—that should revive you!'

As they went out, Bethany was chatting volubly, holding Herbert tightly before putting him to 'bed' in a box Callum had provided. In a few minutes she would have forgotten all about her ordeal.

Lucy looked awkwardly at Callum. 'I'm very grateful. You were marvellous with Bethany. I think I'd better get a Herbert for my room—it's a brilliant idea!'

Callum smiled. 'Perhaps we'd better get a whole family of bears for every contingency!'

They both laughed, their eyes suddenly meeting in mutual humour. Lucy glanced away hastily—she couldn't deal with intimate looks at the moment. The thing was, she told herself sternly, to keep everything light and impersonal, and only to discuss things to do with work—that's where she'd gone wrong before.

'Thanks again,' she said gruffly, and started to walk quickly out of the room.

'Just a minute, Lucy.' Callum's hand shot out and held her arm. 'Can I have a word?'

'Now?'

'It won't take long. I wanted to apologise for what happened earlier. Perhaps I was a little…impetuous! We need to clear the air. I didn't mean anything by it.'

Lucy smiled drily. 'You mean you do that to all the girls?'

'Don't be ridiculous—of course not.' He added gently, 'You had no need to kiss me back if it wasn't what you wanted.'

Her face burned. Callum was right—she had encouraged him, acting just as she'd done when Ben had first seduced her, and how much she regretted that!

His hand was still on her arm and he tightened it slightly, drawing her nearer to him, looking down at her intently. Her heart rate began to increase its pace alarmingly and she disengaged her arm from his grip and stepped back warily. When someone with Callum's looks was too near, it was hard for her to remain objective!

'Whatever I did, I never meant to hurt you… embarrass you.'

'You've just been through a divorce,' she remarked. 'Perhaps you're beginning to test your wings, as it were.'

He frowned. 'That's rubbish! I know I'm a little impulsive sometimes, but kissing you had nothing to do with being on the rebound from my previous wife. I told you—she's in the past now.'

'On to pastures new, then?' suggested Lucy, hating herself for being bitchy but forcing herself to put a distance between them.

'For God's sake, I hope I'm not as cavalier as that. Perhaps the mood of the moment overcame me. The beautiful morning, being near someone…like you. And as I said before, I didn't think you minded too much either,' he murmured.

A pink flush of embarrassment spread over Lucy's cheeks. 'You took me by surprise,' she said lightly. 'As you say, it must obviously have been just a momentary thing—I think we were on a high after delivering the baby.'

'Obviously,' he murmured. His blue eyes had an unreadable look in them. 'Perhaps it would be easier if I found somewhere other than your house to live. Would you like me to leave?'

A tricky question, that, Lucy thought wryly. For her own peace of mind he ought to leave, but part of her wanted the excitement and fun of his presence— and how illogical was that?

'Of course you can't leave,' she answered. 'The town is bursting at the seams—I doubt you'd get a bed. Anyway, it was just a little incident. Surely we can cope with the…situation.'

A droll smile touched the corner of his lips. 'As you say, it was just a little incident—one that we can deal with. I hope, well like to think we could be good friends.'

'Of course, so do I,' Lucy said hastily.

'Then let's start again.' He smiled, those blue eyes holding hers. 'After all, friendship's a very good basis for a working relationship.'

For the first time that day Lucy relaxed. Callum

and she were alike after all in that work was their first priority and he'd made it clear that that was what he wanted.

He looked at his watch. 'What have we got on the agenda today? I really want to get started, get to know the patients, the way the practice runs.'

She turned to the door. 'We'll be having a short meeting this lunchtime so that you can meet some of our other staff. Bunty will get sandwiches and we'll have it in the small conference room. Tilly Prentice, our community nurse, will be giving a report on some of the patients she visits, and the practice manager will talk about general finances. And, of course, Robert Cassidy, my partner, is looking forward to seeing you.'

'Ah, yes, he's been having treatment at a specialist arthritis unit in Edinburgh—is that right?'

'Yes. I think he's feeling a bit better so he's coming in just for a short while.'

Callum nodded briskly. 'Look forward to that—I'll see you later, then.'

There was at least one practice meeting a week for the staff to evaluate treatments and discuss problems regarding their patients—it was essential that everyone involved in their care was kept well informed. Lucy very much wanted this meeting to go well, to show Callum Tate that they were an efficient, caring practice and that their early morning escapade was completely forgotten!

Everyone arrived at once and Lucy wasted no time introducing Callum to Tilly, the community nurse, Vivian Smith, the practice nurse, and Joe Turner, the practice manager.

Tilly smiled at both doctors. 'I've been told you had fun and games last night—everything from delivering babies to flooded roads! A good start to your first day in the practice, Callum.'

Lucy closed her eyes momentarily and felt her cheeks redden. Was there a hidden meaning in Tilly's remarks and had word got round already that they'd been seen in a passionate embrace?

'It was certainly an exciting few hours,' said Callum, seemingly unfazed by Tilly's remark. 'Fortunately the baby arrived with no complications.'

Lucy heaved a sigh of relief as Robert came in. People's attention was diverted to greeting him, and he, too, was introduced to Callum. Then Lucy started the meeting before any more remarks could be made about the previous evening!

Joe Turner gave a quick run-down on their finances and what had been spent on drug usage over the past month. There was a discussion on missed appointments by patients and suggestions as to how to reduce these, and then Tilly expressed her concern about an elderly patient she'd been visiting.

'Florence Woodrow lives in an isolated cottage by the shore,' she explained. 'She's eighty-nine and has had one or two little falls. Luckily her son called to see her by chance the other day when she'd just stumbled, and she seemed to recover quickly. However, when I called to check on her yesterday, she seemed dehydrated and that may have made her slightly disorientated. She insisted to me that she was eating and drinking plenty, but I got the feeling she wasn't looking after herself properly. I do wonder if she's getting near the time when she'll be unable to cope by herself.'

'Knowing Florence, I'm sure she'll want to stay in her own home,' said Lucy. 'She's a very independent lady and has refused all previous offers of help. Why don't we see how she goes on for a little while, with the rapid response team giving her some practical support for a week or so? Perhaps Callum and I could call in this afternoon and see how she is. It would be good to get Callum's assessment of the situation and for her to meet him.'

'I'd like to do that,' he said. 'I'll follow you on my motorbike and then I can do the rest of my visits.'

They all drifted away after the meeting except for Robert, who started up an earnest conversation in one corner with Callum. Tilly Prentice came up to Lucy with her notes on Florence Woodrow.

'These might be useful to have,' she suggested. Then she looked admiringly at Callum. 'Wow!' she murmured to Lucy. 'If I wasn't a happily married woman I'd have serious thoughts about our new doc—he's gorgeous! I can see most of our female patients suddenly needing urgent appointments!'

'He's not bad…' Lucy's voice was casual.

'Not bad? Have you had an eye test recently?'

'I'm more interested in his medical abilities,' retorted Lucy rather pompously.

'I suppose he's married, with dozens of children?' persisted Tilly.

'He's divorced,' said Lucy briefly, looking through some notes and avoiding Tilly's knowing eyes. 'But to change the subject, will you be around at the country show? I know the St John Ambulance people will be there, but it would be good to know you were around as well.'

'Sure I will. The kids are entered for some of the

minor events, so I'll be there most of the time!' Tilly glanced at her watch. 'Must fly now—got a load of visits to get done.'

Lucy went over to Callum and Robert. 'You two seem to have a lot to talk about.' She smiled.

'I've been hearing about Robert's treatment—sounds quite a cocktail of drugs they've got him on!'

Robert chuckled. 'I hope I haven't bored you to death about my damned illness.'

Callum shook his head. 'Don't be ridiculous—I've found it really illuminating. Do you have any physio clinics for rheumatoid and arthritic patients at the surgery?'

'Not as such,' admitted Robert. 'But it's certainly something to consider. I think the physiotherapist we have could easily increase her hours.'

Callum excused himself and left the room to check up on the home visits he was going to do, and Robert smiled at Lucy.

'I think you've found a winner there with Callum. He seems to be just what we're looking for—reliable, knowledgeable and full of good ideas. Let's try and hold onto him as long as we can—I can't see him being a problem!'

'I hope not,' murmured Lucy. 'I really hope not!'

Lucy watched Callum's leather-encased figure roar down the hill towards her as she stood at the little stone-washed cottage standing slightly back from the shoreline where she'd parked the car. The storms of the night before had completely gone, and now it was getting quite warm—beyond the ribbon of golden sands the sea was a sparkling jewel.

Callum skidded to a halt in a spray of gravel, leapt off his bike and pulled off his helmet. Lucy stifled a giggle. He looked liked a modern version of Superman on a mission to save someone! He gave a low whistle and gazed round appreciatively at the scene.

'No wonder you love living here rather than London—it's absolutely beautiful. You'll have to show me around,' he remarked. 'How long have you been here?'

'Nearly four years now. A friend I was at med school with knew I wanted a move, and she was leaving here for a job abroad. I leapt at it.'

'Quite a contrast, working in the wide open spaces, compared to London. Do you miss it at all?'

'I did miss my patients, the friends I'd made...not much else.'

'The social life?'

They crunched their way up the pebble path and Lucy bit her lip. 'Not really,' she said briefly.

She flicked a glance at Callum. She wasn't about to tell him *just* how little she'd missed the social life. Her betrayal by Ben, so unexpected, and of course, even more than that, her betrayal by her father, had coloured the whole of her life down in London and had probably made her wary of men for ever.

'About Florence,' she said, changing the subject to something safer. ' She's a lovely old lady—lived here over fifty years, and still has her peat fire, even in the summer.' She sighed. 'She brought up her family here, and I do hope we can find a suitable solution for her—but it won't be easy.'

'It never is,' remarked Callum. 'Trying to reconcile an individual's wishes with that of her needs can be darn difficult—especially in these days of scattered families.'

'That's absolutely right,' she agreed. 'Florence has three children and only one lives near enough to call occasionally. He's a merchant seaman, so he's away more often than he's here.'

Lucy knocked on the door, and a frenzied barking sounded from the hallway and the noise of an animal flinging itself against the door was heard. Lucy knocked again, slightly louder, and they waited, all the time the dog barking hysterically.

'I don't like the feel of this a bit,' said Lucy. 'I'm sure Florence would have answered the door by now.'

Callum looked through one of the windows at the front, then walked round the back, peering in through the half-closed curtains. In a few moments he ran back, concern on his face.

'I can see Florence lying on the floor in the little kitchen,' he reported. 'There's a pan on the stove and it's boiling its head off—we'll have to get in quickly.'

He stood in front of the door. 'Stand back and I'll have a go at forcing the door open.'

It was a substantial oak door, but after two or three hefty shoves it sprang open and a furious Cairn terrier bounded out, snarling and whining at them both, then snapping at Callum's heels as he pushed his way down the corridor to the back of the house.

'Skeeter! Get down! Come on…be a good dog now.'

Lucy bent down to the little animal and tried to placate it, and gradually it calmed down. It knew Lucy, and the fact she remembered its name was a help! She went into the tiny living room where she knew there was a glass jar full of dog biscuits, which she'd seen Florence feed Skeeter with before, and tossed two or three on the floor. Then she went through to where Callum was kneeling by Florence, his finger feeling the pulse on the carotid artery in her neck.

He looked up. 'She's still with us,' he said quietly. 'But she may have fractured her hip, and I think she's concussed.'

'Oh, no, poor Florence.'

'Lucky we came when we did. There was an egg in the pan, and it had practically boiled dry. Another few minutes and it would probably have exploded!'

Lucy dropped down by the old lady's side and put her mouth close to the woman's ear. 'Florence, Florence…can you hear me?'

They watched and the woman stirred slightly, her eyelids fluttering open. She looked at them dazedly for a moment.

'What's happened to me?' she quavered. 'What have I done?'

'It's all right, Florence, it's me, Dr Cunningham. You've had a fall in the kitchen, and I think you've probably hit your head on the stove and hurt your leg. Is it painful?'

Florence's face grimaced and she sucked in her breath. 'Aye, it is, that. I can't move… Oh, dear…'

Lucy patted the old lady comfortingly on the shoulder. 'Don't worry, love, you'll be all right. We're here to help you, but I think you'll have to go to hospital for a check to see what you've done to yourself.' She indicated Callum, standing beside her. 'This is my new colleague, Dr Tate—he was the one who managed to force the door and get into the cottage.'

Florence's eyes flickered over Callum and she gave a ghost of a smile. 'It's a hefty door, that—good job he's such a strapping lad. He reminds me of my husband—he was a good-looking fellow, too.'

Callum grinned. 'Flattery will get you everywhere, Mrs Woodrow.'

'You're not going to send me away?' The tired old eyes looked fearfully up at the two doctors, and she said weakly, 'If you do, I know they'll never let me back again, will they?'

'You don't know that, Florence. I'm sure once you're better we'll do all we can to keep you in your own home as long as it's possible.'

'It'll be the last time I see my little house—I'm sure of it.' Florence's voice trembled slightly, then she rallied, and said firmly, 'When that nurse came, she said I wasn't feeding myself properly. I don't want to go...'

It was heartbreaking to watch her distress. Lucy held the old woman's hand. 'You mustn't worry too much—there are things we can set in motion, like meals on wheels and a home help. I know you rejected them before, but I think you might enjoy someone else cooking a good meal a day for you!'

Callum took his mobile out of his pocket and touched Lucy on the shoulder. 'I'll ring for an ambulance,' he said quietly. 'That leg looks rotated and a bit shortened, which could mean a fractured neck of femur—and she's obviously in shock.'

He went into the hallway to make the call, and Lucy fetched a pillow from the bedroom as well as a blanket, which she placed gently over the frail figure.

'How can we get hold of your son, Florence? He's not gone back to sea yet, has he?'

The old lady shook her head. 'Not till the week-end—but he's very busy catching up on all his shore work…'

Lucy squeezed Florence's hand. 'He'll not be too busy to come and see his mother—you know that.'

They watched as Florence was stretchered into the ambulance, her mournful little face managing a watery smile.

'Thank you, Doctors,' she whispered. 'It's a good job you came—Skeeter and me could have been there a good few days if you hadn't arrived.' She looked around anxiously. 'What's happened to my little dog? Who'll look after him when I'm gone? He can't be left here!'

'Don't worry,' said Callum with a reassuring smile. 'We'll make arrangements for Skeeter to be looked after—won't we, Dr Cunningham?'

Lucy could hear the dog still barking hysterically in the house. 'Of course,' she said hollowly. 'Won't be a problem!'

As the ambulance disappeared down the road she turned to Callum indignantly. 'Just what arrangements have you in mind for the dog, Doctor?'

'Well,' he said vaguely, 'do you think your cat would mind having a canine friend in the house for a while?'

Lucy laughed. 'If I wasn't eternally grateful to you for being here and getting through that door, I'd tell you to get lost! As it happens, there is a patient further along this road who I think would be pleased to help. She's a lady on her own—used to be a cleaner at the surgery. I saw her the other day, and she mentioned something about wanting a pet. Perhaps she could look after Skeeter and see how she likes that!'

'There you are, then!' Callum said with an air of triumph, 'The arrangements are in place already!'

They wandered out to the car, and the tangy smell of the sea hit their nostrils.

Lucy wrinkled her nose appreciatively. 'Isn't that a lovely fresh smell?' she said. 'Wish I had the rest of the afternoon off to go dolphin-watching instead of holding a diabetic clinic.'

'That sounds a wonderful idea. I didn't know you could do that here. I've seen Australian dolphins, but never Scottish ones!'

Without thinking, Lucy remarked casually, 'Then I'll have to show you some time—on a good day we'd see seals basking on the rocks as well.'

'I'll hold you to that—that's something I'd really love to do.' Callum smiled at her, his fantastic eyes crinkling down at her, alight with pleasure. 'We'll take a picnic and make a day of it. I'll speak to you about that later.'

He pulled on his crash helmet and swung his leg over his motorbike. 'See you—send out a search party if I'm not back by midnight. I'll probably get hopelessly lost, trying to find all these patients scattered over the hills!'

Lucy watched him roar off, her heart still galloping from his electric presence, and sighed. What on earth had compelled her to offer to take him to see the dolphins? They were going to be flung together enough in the house, let alone just the two of them in a small boat! She opened the car door and gazed pensively at the sea before she got in, alarmed that the thought of a day alone with him sent a shiver of excitement mixed with fright through her whole body. She'd thought they'd sorted things out between them earlier. Now she wasn't so sure she could keep her side of the bargain and regard him as just a good friend—not when he sent her whole body into overdrive when he was near her!

'Stop thinking of that darned man,' she said severely to herself, as she drove off to see Mrs Souter to ask if she'd look after Skeeter for a while. 'Perhaps,' she mused optimistically, 'if I see him as little as possible outside the surgery—go to bed before him, get up before him—Callum's attraction will begin to fade.'

But in her heart of hearts she knew that wouldn't happen. However determined she was not to let a man into her life again, she knew that she couldn't just turn off the overwhelming attraction she felt towards him—and Callum was nothing like Ben had been at all.

CHAPTER FIVE

LUCY sat on one of the benches at the side of the big field, watching the preparations for the county show. She hugged her arms round her body as if to keep in check the jumble of emotions that whirled round inside her like the ingredients in a mixer—a concoction of excitement, happiness and anxiety!

A few hours ago life had been as ordinary as ever, spiced slightly by the continuing attraction she felt for Callum. She'd done her best to ensure they met as little as possible out of working hours, being out with friends some nights or staying late at the surgery to do paperwork. Keeping her distance seemed to work quite well. Occasionally they met on the stairs, or discussed things at work—everything seemed pleasant but fairly formal. Despite this, Callum occupied her thoughts far too much, visions of him dancing into her mind at the most untimely occasions. Then suddenly in the last twenty-four hours her life had changed completely. She'd been left in no doubt at all that she was never again going to be able to think of him as just a colleague!

She hardly noticed the knot of people struggling to erect stalls selling local produce and housing small attractions like darts or crockery-smashing. Her eyes were glued to Callum at the other end of the field, tossing some canvas over a frame as easily as throwing a sheet on a bed, then lashing the support guy ropes to the ground. He'd volunteered eagerly to help, obviously wanting to be part of his new community—and already, after only two weeks, he seemed to fit in amazingly well.

Some doctors in new posts found it hard at first to be accepted by patients who had grown to trust and love their old GPs. Callum, reflected Lucy, had had no such difficulty. His sympathetic and assured manner had won the patients over quickly—but she had never anticipated that she, so badly hurt by men in the past, would fall so quickly and unexpectedly under his spell.

The noise of activity in the field and the sound of the local band practising faded into the background as her mind drifted back to what had happened a few hours ago. She couldn't stay out all the time, trying to avoid Callum, and she had come back to the house the previous evening, feeling exhausted after a busy day. A tantalising smell of roast meat cooked in rosemary had drifted towards her as she'd opened the front door.

Callum had been in the kitchen, bending over the stove.

'What are you up to?' she'd asked. 'It smells fantastic—I didn't know you were a cook.'

He'd turned round with a grin. 'I wanted to surprise you—thank you in a small way for offering me shelter for a while. I thought you'd like some home cooking instead of those dreadful low-calorie frozen meals you're always eating. This dish is my pièce de résistance, lamb in a herb crust—nothing better after a hard day's surgery, and I know you've had a very heavy list of visits.'

Lucy's mouth watered and she forgot her determination not to spend too much time with Callum. 'I didn't have time for any lunch today, and I'm starving!' she admitted.

'Glad you're not one of these girls who never eats anything.'

'It's my sister who diets—that's why she has a pencil-slim figure!'

Callum glance wandered slowly over her statuesque form. 'You seem very much OK to me. Your sister ought to think of the example she's setting to her own children—too many seem to have eating disorders these days. Now, sit down and eat this before the chef gets cross!'

It was delicious, together with the red wine he plied her with, and they had a pleasant and relaxed meal, discussing the surgery and local matters. Afterwards Lucy sat back on the sofa, leaning her head against the back and feeling the tensions of the day ease away.

'That was a lovely surprise, Callum. Thank you. I'll sleep like a log tonight.'

He sat down beside her and twirled the brandy, which he'd poured for both of them, round in his glass. 'Sometimes it's nice to spoil oneself,' he murmured.

He looked at her profile, the position of her head emphasising the curve of her slim neck, her silky dark hair spread out like a raven's wing. She was so beautiful, he reflected, and completely unconscious of her own attraction. When she smiled her whole face lit up in animation, her big dark eyes sparkling—but that was when they talked of mundane matters. When personal subjects were alluded to, then too often the expression on her face became closed, unfathomable, perhaps hiding scars of previous unhappiness. Lucy

Cunningham didn't want to get close to anyone.
There were hidden depths about this woman that intrigued and troubled Callum, and he hoped that a relaxed evening together would help him to understand
some of that mystery.

'You know,' he said slowly after a few seconds'
silence, 'you've no need to avoid me when I'm here.
I get the impression that you've been doing anything
rather than stay in your own house out of working
hours!'

Lucy felt her cheeks redden. 'Don't be silly—of
course I haven't. I've just been busy.'

He looked at her quizzically. 'Your life is your own
and I don't want to pry—but what are you frightened
of, Lucy?'

The stark question took her by surprise and she sat
up, twisting her hands together in confusion. 'What
do you mean? Why should I be frightened?'

His hand held her chin gently and turned her face
to his. 'I don't know the precise reason—but I do
know that whenever we're in the same room you're
as taut as a bowstring. I'm not an ogre, you know. I
won't hurt you—and I would like to know you better.
After all, didn't we decide that we should be friends
as well as colleagues?'

'Wh-what do you want to know?' Lucy shivered,
feeling trapped as every nerve in her body vibrated
at the touch of his hand, nervous at the personal nature of his questions.

He had not taken his hand from her face, but traced
the line of her chin with his finger, his deep blue eyes
holding hers. 'You are so...beautiful,' he murmured.
'There must have been many men who have loved

you—but something or someone has made you wary of any close relationship. Am I right?'

She tried to move away, treat his remarks with dignified aloofness, but her limbs felt heavy, the wine and brandy making her slow to react.

'I don't know what you mean,' she said feebly. 'Of course I've had boyfriends...'

He moved nearer, frowning slightly, and his voice was dismissive. 'I'm talking of something more than boyfriends. I guess, Lucy, that you have had a great love in your life and you've been hurt in some way.'

Lucy shifted her gaze and looked down at her hands. What did he want her to do, she thought bitterly, admit that the two men she'd loved most of all in her life had both let her down most cruelly? For a while her life had been a nightmare, and she didn't know if she wanted to tell that story. What good would it do to reveal how she'd been betrayed?

She shut her eyes and tried to squeeze out the picture that still sprang so easily and horrifyingly into her mind even after three years. It was like the rewinding of some horrible video, every detail shown vividly before her. She recalled opening the door of the bedroom and gazing incredulously for a minute at the sight before her. Her eyes hadn't made sense of what they'd been seeing, then gradually her vision had cleared and she'd realised that it had been Ben, whom she'd loved so much and had thought loved her, lying entwined with Gina, her older stepsister, on the bed. He had been waving a cheque in the air, his well-bred voice triumphant.

'Got the dosh, Gina, darling. Good old Lucy coughed up quite easily. We can get that little business going now...'

They hadn't realised she was standing there at first, then they turned and both looked at her, transfixed. For a second their eyes locked in mutual horror, then Lucy slammed the door so hard as she left that the pictures fell off the wall.

The tears, so often near the surface when she could bring herself to think about that horrible incident, rolled slowly down her cheeks and she clenched her teeth to try and stop them. Callum would think she was mad—still affected after all these years!

He gave a sharp intake of breath as he saw her distress. 'What is it? What have I said? Oh, sweetheart, what a blundering fool I am. I didn't mean to upset you… Here…' He scrabbled in his pocket and produced a handkerchief. 'Let me wipe those tears away.'

He dabbed her face gently. 'I touched a nerve there, didn't I? Forgive me—I've always said too much, jumped in too quickly, as you heard before. I'm a clumsy idiot!'

Somehow his arms came around her and her head was against his chest as he patted her back as one would a child. She heard the comforting solid beat of his heart against her ear, and gradually she became calmer, the images she'd called to mind fading.

'Don't worry,' she sniffled, 'I do feel better now— and it's not your fault that Ben was a complete rat!'

'Ben?'

'Ben Marston—he's an actor, though not very successful, and I met him through Jan, my sister. He…he seemed to love me and we set up home together. He didn't have much money—he ''rested'' quite a lot, as they say, so I was quite happy to pay the rent until he got a good job.'

'You supported him, then?'

'Yes,' admitted Lucy.

His arms tightened round her. 'And now you're going to tell me that he bled you dry and then went off with someone else?'

She looked at Callum, astonished. 'How did you know?'

He gave a harsh laugh. 'Because it happens all the time, as I know from experience. I'm right, am I?'

Lucy shivered. 'I'm afraid so—and the way I found out wasn't very pleasant. You see, I found him in bed with Gina, my stepsister, and they were celebrating the fact that because of me he could afford to start some venture with her!'

'Lord,' whispered Callum. 'Your stepsister! What a thing to find out...'

'It was my fault. I was naïve, too trusting. I fell for him so hard that it blinded me to his obvious faults.'

'You mustn't blame yourself—that's ridiculous. You've had a lucky escape, I'd say.'

'I know,' admitted Lucy in a small voice.

He smiled gently down at her, still holding her close in his arms. 'And that's why you're wary of men, is it?'

'Wouldn't you be? He's not the only man in my life to have let me down...but that's another story.' Her voice was muffled as she whispered into his chest, 'It'll be a long time before I trust a man again...'

'Of course you will!' His chin was against her forehead, and his voice reverberated through her skull. 'Don't let that scumbag spoil your life—you've got to start enjoying yourself again!'

'It was such a shock, you see,' Lucy explained.

'But in my heart of hearts perhaps I knew he didn't love me as I did him—I just didn't expect it to be demonstrated quite so graphically!'

She looked so woebegone. He brushed her forehead with his lips and stroked her hair gently. 'I want to see you carefree again, Lucy—you can't change the past, so think of the future!'

How kind he was, and how surprisingly easy it had been after all to tell him her pathetic little story. Lucy looked up at him gratefully. She didn't feel awkward being held so very close—it just felt comfortable and comforting. It was strange that now she'd related her background she felt a curious sense of release, almost as if she'd closed a chapter on her life.

Callum drew her closer to him. 'Don't let it spoil your life—you must move on,' he said, his voice firm. 'Perhaps I understand how you feel more than many people would, but you must forget about it.'

His face was so close to hers. She could see his black lashes fringing those sexy, humorous eyes, the evening stubble on his chin, feel his breath on her cheek. It felt so natural that his mouth should move from her forehead to her lips, kissing them gently at first, then passionately with a fierce hunger, teasing them open, fluttering down her jawline to the little hollow in her neck.

It was all happening far too quickly, but she didn't care any more, because for the first time in years she gave herself up to the sensations coursing through her body. Callum was right—why should she allow a man who broke her heart a long time ago to dominate her life now? Why deny herself pleasure with a man who she was sure was trustworthy and would never lie to her for his own gain—the complete antithesis of Ben?

She moaned softly with pleasure and his body was hard and tense against hers as she returned his kisses and pressed herself against him longingly, every nerve end tingling.

He smiled tenderly down at her. 'Gently, sweetheart—we have a lot of time!'

'I don't want to wait,' she whispered. 'Kiss me again.'

Their bodies seemed almost welded together, hip to hip, and she could feel only too clearly his need of her. His kisses became more demanding, plundering her mouth, his hands exploring her body so that she twisted and wriggled in exquisite delight.

Then suddenly he drew back a little, his eyes questioning. 'Are you sure this is what you want, Lucy?' His voice was ragged and urgent. 'Are you going to be sorry later? Soon we may be past the point of no return...'

She laughed throatily, and touched his cheek. 'Perhaps I'm mad but, yes, this is what I want—I want to enjoy life, like you said, and I want...I want you to help me do that...' Her eyes laughed up at his, sure of herself for the first time. 'We know each other better than that first time we kissed—and don't good friends help each other when they can?'

He grinned. 'I'll do my very best,' he promised, and then he lifted her bodily in his arms, took her up the stairs and laid her on her bed.

She gazed up at him in the half-light of the bedroom, examining the face of this man she'd known for such a little while. Two weeks ago he had virtually declared he wanted no relationships in his life—had he changed as much as she had? Somehow they'd reached a watershed and she didn't want him to feel trapped.

'Look,' she said urgently, 'don't think of this as a commitment—there's no strings attached.'

His eyes darkened. 'Then let's enjoy the moment, my sweet,' he murmured, gently removing her clothes until she lay naked before him.

Then all she remembered was his hard and demanding body on her soft skin, his skilful hands arousing her to fever pitch, and a feeling of complete joy.

'So how are we today?'

Lucy blinked, the sounds of the present moment crowding back on her—the wind whistling through the trees, men shouting and children calling. Before her stood Callum, his strong muscular legs in old khaki shorts, his face spattered with mud, laughter dancing in his eyes, and she felt waves of happiness ripple through her again. She had no doubts now—surely a man couldn't make love to a girl like he had and not feel something for her?

'I feel fine—rather good, in fact,' she replied primly.

'And why should that be?' Callum teased.

She stifled a giggle. 'Because I slept so well last night!'

'I'm not surprised,' he said softly. 'I hope it's the first of many nights like that…'

They gazed at each other, both overwhelmed for a moment by the thought of future love-making together. Callum put his hand behind her neck and pulled her towards him.

'I could make love to you right now,' he whispered

fiercely. 'I can't wait to feel that beautiful body next to mine…'

'Callum! Don't do that here—it'll be all round the town…'

His hand slipped down around her waist. 'So what?'

Lucy slipped from his grasp. 'We must be discreet for the moment…the patients might not approve. After all, you're only supposed to be living with me because of the flooded flat. Once they think we're living together for…other reasons, there might be a few raised eyebrows in this community when you've only been here two weeks!'

His hand dropped away and he gave a theatrical sigh. 'You're right, I suppose. But it doesn't stop me wanting you…I hope I can last out till this evening!'

One of the men who'd been erecting the stalls came up and Lucy greeted him and introduced him to Callum. 'This is Ian Curtis,' she said. 'He's been sorting out the flood at the flat.'

'Aye, that's been done—it meant a new tank, of course, but apart from some decorating, the doctor can move back in again.'

'Oh, dear…are you sure?' Lucy bit her lip—that had sounded a little strange, and she heard Callum give a low chuckle. 'I mean, that's all that needs doing, is it?' she added hastily.

'Oh, yes—the structure all seems sound. They built things well in those days!'

'So can you get a decorator—and, if so, how long will it take?'

Ian pursed his lips. 'My son-in-law can do it. He's a bit strapped for time—he's been asked to be on hand to do some work for the film crew that's staying here—but I'll ask him to do it as soon as possible.'

'No hurry,' remarked Callum easily. 'I wouldn't want him to rush things!'

'Could be a week or so before he's finished, though...'

'What a terrible shame,' murmured Callum as Ian wandered back over the field. 'Looks like you'll have to put up with me for a while longer.' He glanced up at the sky. 'And it looks like the weather's improving—it's getting quite hot so there should be a crowd of visitors.'

Lucy nodded. 'I'll stay here and watch some of the racing. I've got to be around in case I'm needed.'

Callum caught her arm. 'Don't go far,' he murmured, his lips just brushing hers in a quick gesture that sent her stomach fluttering as if there were a thousand butterflies there. 'I'm going to have a go at some of these competitions—but tonight we'll go for a walk, have a drink at a pub somewhere. I think we deserve a celebration, don't you?'

Their eyes locked, and Lucy nodded silently, hardly able to speak for the happiness welling up inside her. Everything had happened so quickly and there was still lots she wanted to know about Callum, but she had all the time in the world to find out! He might not have mentioned commitment yet, but Ben had strung her along with a load of promises that he hadn't kept. Callum had promised nothing, but she trusted him not to betray her. She was having a passionate affair with the most drop-dead gorgeous man in the world and going to enjoy every minute!

Lucy settled down on a chair to watch Tilly Prentice's twin little boys take part in some of the races on the outside track. A multitude of things were taking place in the space inside—several powerful-looking men were hurling huge weights over high poles and on a stage nearby, a group of young girls was dancing neatly, their kilts swinging, legs flashing. Every now and then a loud voice would bellow information indistinctly through a loudspeaker, and in the background the jolly sounds of a small fairground could be heard.

Tilly flopped down beside her, her slim figure dressed in striking pink cropped trousers and a matching fitted top. 'I'm exhausted,' she said, resting her head against the back of the chair. 'Getting Liam and Keiron ready for anything is a feat in itself, and then the darned dog had to run away just as we were about to set off. I've certainly no energy for the mothers' race!'

'That's not like you, Tilly—you're usually up for anything.' Lucy frowned as she looked at her friend. 'Have you lost weight?' she asked, suddenly noticing how loosely Tilly's trousers seemed to hang on her. 'You've not been dieting, have you?'

Tilly shrugged. 'Might have lost a bit,' she admitted. 'But it's more to do with rushing round than anything else—and the fact is I don't feel very hungry. Too much food seems to make me feel sick these days—but it's nothing.' She peered round at the field. 'I see Callum's having a go at hurling those weights—hope he doesn't strain anything!'

'So do I,' murmured Lucy, giving a dissatisfied glance at her friend. 'Look, Tilly, I think you ought to let me examine you. You've mentioned a few symptoms that ought to be investigated—I don't want our community nurse to go on the blink!'

'Don't be such an old woman,' retorted Tilly. 'I've got two exhausting children and a job—it's natural to be tired. Don't forget I'm not a complete ignoramus—if I think I need looking at, I'll tell you!'

'Sorry, madam!' Lucy grinned. 'I defer to your superior knowledge!'

They both sat back and watched the activities on the field for a moment, then Tilly said admiringly, 'You know, that Callum's a great guy. All the patients love him. Do you think he's enjoying it here?'

Lucy tried to suppress a giggle. 'Oh, I think he is at the moment, very much…or so he's told me!'

'He's certainly a hit with the patients. I went to see Florence Woodrow in hospital yesterday to see what progress she's making. She couldn't stop talking about how he'd rescued her. It's funny,' she mused. 'You'd have thought a man like that would be spoken for. I wonder what went wrong in his marriage? He seems such an easygoing man.'

'I don't really know,' replied Lucy briefly, but she couldn't help blushing, her cheeks dimpling in a wide happy smile.

Tilly stared at her searchingly. 'If I didn't know you better, Lucy Cunningham, I'd say there was something going on!' she said slowly. Leaning forward in her chair, she laughed. 'I've hit the bull's-eye, haven't I? You and superman Callum Tate are an item, right? And I thought you were under the same roof because you'd offered him shelter until the flat was put right!'

'But that's what did happen—everywhere else is booked up,' protested Lucy, then she caught Tilly's sceptical eye. 'That's how it started anyway,' she said feebly.

'But things have progressed—you're more than just good friends now?' teased Tilly.

It was no use denying it. After all, how could they keep it quiet in the small confines of the practice? And someone was bound to see them together.

'I suppose you could say so,' she admitted with a grin. 'But don't tell the whole world!'

Tilly patted her arm. 'I'm so pleased for you—I really am. About time you had a nice bloke!'

'It's early days yet, of course...' said Lucy cautiously. 'Don't imagine that we'll be walking up the aisle soon.'

'My lips are sealed,' promised Tilly.

Lucy flicked a look at Tilly's casual but stylish attire. It hadn't seemed to matter before Callum had come into her life, but she was beginning to feel rather frumpish and old-fashioned in comparison. Perhaps she ought to make more of herself—this new optimistic life demanded clothes that weren't over three years old and more fun than the few outfits that she had for work.

'Tilly, can I ask you something? Where do you get your clothes? You can't have found them in the shops round here—they're far too smart. Everything I've got seems to be falling to pieces and I've no time to wander round, looking.'

Tilly grinned. 'New life, new image, eh? I get all mine from a rather good catalogue, and I'll lend it you with pleasure.' She laughed. 'To be honest, someone with your figure and looks deserves some sparky clothes—you'd show them off wonderfully. About time you spent some money on yourself.'

'I think you're right,' murmured Lucy.

There was a shrill whistle and a crowd of little boys scampered past them, encouraged by shouting parents. Liam and Keiron seemed to be at the forefront and in a few minutes appeared with beaming smiles and little medals strung round their necks.

'Look, Mummy, we got medals!' they shouted, jumping up and down and then turning cartwheels to demonstrate their excitement. 'Now come and be in your race—please!'

They hauled Tilly up on her feet, and with a resigned look at Lucy she allowed herself to be taken to the starting line.

Lucy watched the two little figures dragging their mother along, like two little ducklings, and gave a small sigh. Dare she look too far ahead, dare she even imagine that one day she and Callum might have children? Then she frowned. She had to stop thinking like that—Callum Tate had just come out of a divorce and wasn't likely to be thinking long term at the moment. She was going into this relationship with no promises made, just living life for the present with a wonderful man.

The loudspeaker was informing everyone in muffled tones that the hill race was about to start on the lower slopes of the hill that formed such a wonderful backdrop to the games. Lucy squinted up the slope. She could see the flags that marked out the route, and it seemed a long way up, although she knew that it only took the contestants about quarter of an hour to complete it. In the warm sun she began to drift off to sleep, pleasantly exhausted by the emotional turmoil of the night before.

It was the sound of her mobile going off in her pocket that startled her to wakefulness.

'St John Ambulance tent here, Dr Cunningham. Could you come, please? We've got a young lad here who can't seem to get his breath. He's just been brought down from the hill run and we're worried about him.'

Lucy strode quickly over the field to the tent. It was to be expected that there'd be a few casualties on a day like this, but she'd rather hoped that it would be a trouble-free afternoon, allowing her to daydream about her and Callum!

Shona Cameron, stout and capable, and encased in a tight St John's uniform, met Lucy with a worried look.

'It's young Stevie Richards,' she said in a low voice. 'I've propped him up on the bed with some pillows and he's taken his Ventolin—but it doesn't seem to be having any effect.'

Lucy bent down beside the youth, one professional glance taking in his unnatural pallor and the tinge of blue around his lips. His thin chest, covered by a sin-glet, heaved up and down, trying to force air into lungs that were already expanded. The tent was filled with the wheezing, whistling sound of the choked-up tubes in his lungs trying to expel air, interspersed with a dry, harsh cough. He was a patient at the practice and he had a history of mild asthma.

'Hello, Stevie,' she said in a calm voice, disguising any concern she felt about his condition. 'You seem to be rattling away rather a lot. This came on during the hill race, I take it?'

Stevie nodded mournfully. 'I've not had an attack for ages,' he gasped.

'Don't worry—we'll have you breathing easier very soon.'

Lucy picked up his wrist and felt the galloping pulse rate. Thank God she'd come earlier and ensured that the tent was stocked with most of the basic emergency equipment that might be needed on a day like this.

She attached a pulse oximeter to the boy's finger just as Callum strode into the tent, exuding confidence with his reassuring physical presence.

'I saw this young man being helped across the field,' he said. 'Came to see if you needed any help.'

'Am I glad to see you,' murmured Lucy gratefully. 'The oximeter's telling me his oxygen sats are only 93 per cent and his pulse is over l40. No need to listen to his chest—you can hear it from here!'

'Doesn't sound too good,' he replied briskly. 'I'll call for an ambulance to take him to Ballachter General now to be on the safe side. He'll need his blood gases checked. Have you got a nebuliser?'

'It's a bit ancient, but it should help him for a while. Shona, can you pull over that machine and hook the mask over Stevie's face?'

Gradually the boy's stertorous breathing began to die down and the blue of his lips to fade. He lay back against his pillows looking exhausted and white but perceptibly better.

'Are you feeling more comfortable?' asked Lucy. 'Don't try and move. Dr Tate, my new colleague, is getting an ambulance which will take you to Ballachter General.'

Stevie struggled to sit up, scowling. 'I can't go to hospital, I'm taking an exam on Monday. It's really important!'

'You'll probably be out by then—but there's no way I'm letting you go home until you've been reassessed and monitored.'

The boy looked stubbornly at her. 'I tell you, I'm not going. Last time I was in hospital I had to stay for ages and this exam's really important...to my father anyway.'

'And so is your health.' Callum appeared in the tent doorway. His voice was authoritative without being aggressive. 'If you're wheezing on Monday like you were just now, there's no way you'll be able to sit down to an exam.'

There was a flurry of activity by the entrance, and a large man in a tweed jacket pushed his way forward.

'What the hell's going on? I hear Stevie had to stop running in the race for some reason.'

A sullen expression crossed Stevie's face. 'Hello, Dad. You didn't have to come, you know.'

'I had to find out why you gave up—you were nearly at the finishing line.'

'I...I couldn't get my breath,' muttered the boy mutinously.

'Ah, Mr Richards—you're Stevie's father, aren't you?' asked Lucy politely.

'Yes, I am. What's the matter with him?' The man's voice was aggressive and loud.

'Stevie's had an asthma attack, brought on by exercise. We've called an ambulance to take him to the hospital for monitoring.'

'Asthma? Through exercise? Nonsense! The boy's run plenty of races without trouble before—he just suffers from it mildly. Anyway, he looks fine—he's not wheezing or anything. He should have pushed through the pain barrier and pressed on. You're becoming a wimp, lad!'

'You try and run when you can't breathe—but there's no point in getting you to understand.'

There was something bitter about Stevie's hoarse voice, as if he'd given up hoping his father would sympathise. Lucy met Callum's eyes briefly—it seemed as if Stevie's father would only believe what he wanted to.

'He looks better because he's used a salbutomol nebuliser,' she explained. 'It acts quite quickly to reduce the swelling in his tubes. But he still needs to go and be monitored—his chest isn't right yet.'

'Absolute rubbish! Stevie's got an important exam on Monday—could affect his chances of a good university place. We'll look after him at home, though it seems hardly necessary to me…'

Callum stood by the boy and looked stonily at his father. 'If you take him home now, without further treatment, he may have another attack that could well be much worse than the one he's just experienced. As I told Stevie before, he might well be allowed home tomorrow—but to prevent him going to hospital might mean he'll be too ill to do anything on Monday. It could be very serious.'

There was something about Callum's tone that seemed to cow the aggressive Mr Richards, and he lost some of his bluster.

'Well…I suppose you know best,' he allowed grudgingly. 'But I think it's all a fuss about nothing. They'd better damn well get him better by tomorrow. I haven't spent all this money on his education for it to be thrown away.'

'Perhaps you'd like to go with your son?' suggested Lucy, incredulous at the father's attitude to his son's health. 'You can address any questions you might have then to the chest consultant or one of his team.'

Mr Richards shrugged. 'I don't suppose I'll get anything out of them. They're a breed apart—doctors,' he grumbled as he followed the paramedics carrying Stevie out to the ambulance.

Shona looked at both doctors in disbelief. 'Can you credit it?' she demanded. 'That poor young man—no sympathy from his father at all! Stevie looked really ill…'

'He was ill,' said Callum grimly. 'Asthma can be a killer if it's ignored. Mr Richards seems to be a tad ignorant, and I hope it's made plain to him at the hospital that it's to be taken seriously.'

'It's a good job you were so prompt, Shona,' added Lucy. 'He was actually in a lot of distress. I hope nothing else serious turns up, but let me know if it does.'

The two doctors wandered out into the field again. 'Glad I didn't have a father like that,' remarked Callum. 'He must be hard to live with. His father seems rather too ambitious for his son.'

'Yes,' agreed Lucy a little sadly. 'I imagine he does love Stevie, though. At least he's there for him, even if he is an aggressive pig!'

Callum looked down at Lucy perceptively. 'And yours wasn't there, you mean?'

Lucy shook her head, then gave a short laugh. 'I don't care any more—as you said, that's all behind me now.'

'Quite right,' murmured Callum, putting an arm round her shoulders. 'Let the fun begin! I'll meet you back at the house around seven o'clock and we'll go for that walk and meal I promised.'

And Lucy's heart sang, because she was sure that he was right and the future held many things that she and Callum would do together. There *was* life after heartache!

CHAPTER SIX

LUCY glanced covertly at the official-looking letter which had arrived that morning addressed to Callum. It had an Australian stamp on it, and she wondered if it was the letter of recommendation for Callum—if so, it was a bit late! In fact, she'd already had an email to the effect that Dr Tate was one of the best medics they'd ever had and they had been sorry to lose him. She smiled to herself. How much had happened since that night she'd met Callum at her sister's—it seemed a lifetime ago.

'Letter for you, Callum,' she said, handing it to him as he came down to grab a cup of coffee before dashing out to take the Tuesday morning surgery. He picked the letter up without comment but looked at it with a frown before stuffing it into his jacket pocket.

'Bye, my lovely.' He grinned. 'See you later…'

His hands went under her silk dressing-gown and drew her to him. 'Don't bother changing when I'm out,' he murmured against her neck. 'It won't be worth it…'

She slapped his cheek lightly. 'What are you like, Dr Tate?' She laughed. 'Go away and heal the sick!'

She watched him go, roaring off on his bike, grateful that it was a rare Tuesday morning off and that she didn't have a surgery until after lunch. She picked up the large parcel that had arrived for her and took it up to the bedroom, spreading the contents out on the bed.

'Did I really order all these things from Tilly's catalogue?' she murmured, looking in amazement at the mound of jumpers, suits and trousers she'd taken out of the parcel.

The photographs of cool-looking models in fantastic clothes had obviously gone to her head and there were more outfits on the bed now than she'd bought in three years! She held up against herself a printed dress with a nipped-in waist and short flirty skirt and made a face. It might have looked fantastic in the photographs, but it did nothing for her!

She was going to be in a jam if all the clothes turned out to be mistakes—in a fit of madness she'd thrown away all her old casual clothes and had just assumed that the new ones would suit her.

'You must be a complete idiot,' she told herself crossly as she tried on and rejected another top and skirt that made her look like a schoolgirl. 'You've been conned into thinking you can ever look as good as those models!'

Then she pulled on a pair of cream silk pants and a black top with shoestring straps, and gazed at her image in the mirror with a surprised grin.

'Doesn't look like Dr Lucy Cunningham at all,' she remarked to the image she saw before her. 'More like a dolly bird—but it does have something about it!'

Now she was going out so much more—and with a man she realised she'd fallen head over heels in love with—buying and wearing clothes seemed much more fun, worth doing. She giggled, wondering what her family, let alone Callum, would think of the new-style Lucy who used to have no time for clothes or fashion! She sighed a little wistfully. Her life had changed radically over the few weeks Callum had been with her. She didn't want him to make false promises like Ben had, but sometimes when he held her to him at night she wondered if he'd ever feel able to commit fully to her. Then she shrugged. At the moment she was happy as she was. She trusted him to tell the truth and, as he had told her to, she was enjoying the moment!

She heard the front door open. Callum had returned. He ran up the stairs and came into the bedroom then stopped, his eyes wide.

'Wow,' he said appreciatively, giving a low whistle. 'Don't you look good? Another side to Dr Cunningham, I think!'

'Like it?' Lucy gave a little twirl. 'I've gone completely berserk, ordering all these clothes from Tilly's catalogue...'

Callum caught her round her waist and nuzzled her neck. 'That's good—about time you spoilt yourself a bit. Have you bought anything suitable to wear for an evening out tonight? I thought we'd do something a bit special as I've had a bit of news.'

Lucy looked at him intrigued. 'What kind of news? I hope it's good.'

There seemed to be a peculiar twinkling light in his eyes, his expression at once mysterious and animated. A smile played round his lips. 'All in good time, sweetheart—you'll find out soon enough. I just dashed in between home visits to make sure you knew that we'd be going out.'

'But I want to know what kind of clothes to wear,' she protested.

'Surprise me!' was his unhelpful remark. He pulled her against him and kissed her full on her lips, his hands curving possessively over her before pushing her gently away with a sigh. 'Don't tempt me,' he murmured. 'I must go now, before I forget what I should be doing. See you later.'

The surgery was full as usual, and Tilly was sitting on a chair in the office, looking rather pale.

'I thought I was doing dressings on some of our leg patients with ulcers this afternoon,' she remarked forlornly to Lucy. 'I must be mad—Bunty tells me I did them yesterday!'

'I wouldn't have thought you could have forgotten something like that,' said Lucy. 'It's not a job I'd relish. Perhaps it's the heat that's made you forgetful.' She looked more closely at Tilly, noticing the dark shadows under her eyes and her pale face. 'You do look very tired, you know.'

'I could go to sleep for a week,' admitted Tilly. 'No wonder I keep forgetting things. I even forgot the twins' parents' evening last night, and I'm sure there's all sorts of questions I should be asking their teacher!'

She passed a weary hand over her forehead and Lucy frowned, alarm bells ringing in her head. 'How long have you had those marks on your arm?' she asked, touching some rings of redness marking Tilly's upper arm.

Tilly looked at the curious marks, and shrugged. 'I did notice them the other day—they seem to have got bigger since then. Why?'

'I'm not sure,' replied Lucy slowly, 'but there's something odd about them that worries me.' Then with sudden decision she said, 'I won't take no for an answer this time Tilly—I'm going to examine you right now and take some blood tests!'

'You've got that ghastly Mr Richards in the waiting room—isn't he the father of that boy who had asthma at the country show? He won't like being kept waiting!'

'I won't keep him long—but I've seen you looking awful over the last few weeks since the country show, and I don't care what you say—we're going to get to the bottom of this!'

She fixed Tilly with a stern eye, and together they went into her room. 'Now, sit down and tell me honestly how you feel,' Lucy commanded.

Tilly did as she was told and sighed. 'Well, the truth is, I do feel pretty grim. Apart from the tiredness, in the last few weeks I've had various things that seem to have come on at different times, from headaches to thrush, and sometimes every joint in my body aches.' She gave a short laugh. 'Apart from those symptoms, I seem to be more absent-minded than usual—but I put that down to being forty. It seemed mad to complain of odd disparate symptoms, especially as we've just been on holiday.'

Lucy took out a needle and syringe and held Tilly's arm as she prepared to take some blood for tests. 'Where was it you went? I've forgotten,' she asked.

'We went to a cousin of mine who has a holiday house north of here,' said Tilly. 'It was fabulous. The weather was good, and we rode horses and bikes and saw deer and wild birds. I thought Liam and Keiron would be bored, but they loved it.'

Lucy took her blood pressure and listened to her chest. 'Your BP's slightly low,' she said, 'but nothing to worry about. However, I'm sure there's something not quite right. I'll send off these bloods and hopefully we'll get the results back fairly soon.'

'Thanks,' said Tilly in a funny quavering voice. 'It's such a relief to know that I'm not going completely mad, that you think I've might have some genuine lurgy.'

'Trust your own instincts, Tilly—you know your body better than anyone. You should have allowed me to look at you before. You know I wouldn't have laughed at you.'

'OK, OK.' Tilly grinned. 'I'm a naughty girl.' She paused by the door and looked back mischievously at Lucy, more like her old self. 'By the way, you look as if you've still got stars in your eyes! I take it Dr Gorgeous is still in favour?'

'Mind your own business,' said Lucy with a smile. 'And now—can you send in the delightful Mr Richards?'

Pensively tapping her pencil on the desk, Lucy watched Tilly walk out. Something was niggling at the back of her mind regarding Tilly's symptoms, but she couldn't put her finger on it. Later on she'd delve into the matter—right now she had to deal with a red-faced and perspiring Mr Richards. He was still wearing a thick tweed suit, although the weather was hot.

'How can I help you?' asked Lucy, wondering that he didn't expire in the heat.

He sat down heavily on the chair in front of the desk and looked uncharacteristically sheepish, running a finger round his collar.

'I have a little problem,' he said haltingly, and gave a nervous laugh. 'Silly, really, but I seem to have to, er, pass water more than usual—almost every half-hour. It's becoming rather a nuisance.'

Lucy nodded impassively. Funny how big blustering men like Mr Richards found discussing any untoward function of their body with a doctor embarrassing, but they could be as rude and aggressive as possible when in a situation that didn't involve their own health.

'This is a very common problem, Mr Richards—especially in men of your age and older. I see from our notes that you're sixty. It could be that your prostate gland has enlarged and is pressing on the tube leading from the bladder—which obviously means it's difficult to empty and therefore you need to urinate more often.'

'Is it dangerous?'

'Not as such, but it must be investigated. I can give you drugs to try and reduce the size of the gland, or if that isn't successful you might eventually have an operation. The main concern, however, is to check for prostate cancer.'

The man looked shocked. 'Cancer?'

'Don't get too alarmed—it's something we just want to make sure about. We do this initially with a PSA test—a blood test—together with other tests. If they're normal, that indicates a benign prostate enlargement rather than cancer. You'll also need an internal examination.'

'I see,' he said abruptly. 'Well, you'd better take some blood, then. Perhaps I'd should give up work for the moment. I might make it worse by over doing it.'

Lucy suppressed a smile as she tore open the sterile pack containing the needle and syringe for his blood sample. Was this the man who'd told his son he was a wimp not to finish a race while he was having an asthma attack?

'No, Mr Richards, you can carry on as usual. Keep

drinking plenty of water, however. Sometimes men drink as little as possible so that they don't have to keep going to the loo—and that can lead to kidney infection.'

An abject look of fright crossed Mr Richard's face as he watched Lucy search for a vein in his arm and prepare to put the needle in. 'Oh, no,' he whispered. 'Is this going to hurt? Can't you do the test some other way?'

'Look the other way,' commanded Lucy brusquely. 'And, no, I can't do it another way and, no, it won't hurt—there! I've finished.'

Pale and shaken, the man pulled down his shirt-sleeve. 'Never did like that kind of thing,' he muttered. 'Can I go now?'

'Make an appointment for next week and we'll review the results of your blood tests. By the way, is Stevie keeping well after his hospital admission?'

He scowled. 'Right as rain—I knew he would be. Of course, he missed the exam, for no reason at all that I could see. He's got to pull himself together, that boy—makes a fuss about everything!'

As Lucy entered his notes into the computer she reflected wryly that if the boy did make a fuss, he was only following the example of his father!

Bunty came in as Mr Richards left. 'Thought you might like this coffee before you tackle the rest of the list you've got this afternoon—it's humungous!' She paused at the door, her round face registering concern. 'Dr Tate rang to say to be ready for your appointment at seven o'clock this evening. I think it's terrible you have to work in the evening as well after a busy day.'

Lucy didn't put Bunty right regarding the exact nature of the evening. At the moment the receptionist was ignorant of any relationship between them other than a professional one—only Tilly was privileged with that information!

A thrill of anticipation seared through her as she sipped her coffee. In dealing with Mr Richards she'd forgotten the 'special' evening that Callum had mentioned. Just what was this 'news' he was going to tell her? He'd looked incredibly mysterious and she burned with curiosity, wishing like mad that she didn't first have to get through a list which suggested that she'd have patients with complaints as diverse as bunions and anaemia!

It was quite late as Lucy drove up to her house—she'd just have time to bath and change into one of her new outfits before she and Callum went on this mysterious 'special' evening. One thing, she thought firmly to herself, she would not be going as a pillion passenger on that bike of his! He wasn't yet home so she had time for a leisurely and steaming hot bath, soaking luxuriously in the lavender-scented water and reflecting happily how lucky she was to have this wonderful man...

She looked critically at the choice of clothes lying on the bed—if Callum said it was a special evening, then she'd better look special! She slipped on a soft tangerine-coloured silk dress that had come in the parcel and regarded herself doubtfully. The model in the photograph was pencil thin—on Lucy the dress seemed to emphasise the soft swell of her breasts and the silk material clung rather revealingly over her curves. But the colour suited her dark looks, and on a warm balmy evening like this it was cool and comfortable.

'Yes, you'll do!' Callum's deep voice from the door made her jump. He strode forward and held her shoulders, looking down at the dress and taking in the creaminess of her skin against the soft colour.

'That,' he said huskily, 'looks stunning.' His eyes darkened and his hands tightened his hold on her. 'I hope the evening lives up to your expectations, my darling.'

'I don't know what to expect.' She smiled. 'Is this outfit OK, or should I be wearing jeans and a vest top?'

'I told you—you look stunning, and that's all that matters.'

'I wish you'd stop all this cloak-and-dagger stuff,' said Lucy as she followed him down the path to where a taxi waited for them. 'Where are we going to?'

She soon found out—it was a small fish restaurant that had recently been opened next to the little bay where the fishermen came in. There were a few chairs and tables set out on the wide pavement under a jaunty green and white awning. Beyond the bay was the sea, as still as a millpond, and the backdrop of mountains and a sky that was maturing into a series of red and azure blue.

Lucy drew a deep breath. How beautiful it was, and what a lifetime away from the bustle of London. No wonder she had found a peace and calm of mind over the past three years of living here.

'I bet you're ready for this,' said Callum as he poured champagne into her glass. 'I know you had a full list this afternoon.'

Lucy sipped it gratefully, feeling the bubbles

prickle her throat and a pleasant easing of the day's tension flow through her.

'Why the champagne—are we celebrating something?'

'Wait and see,' he teased. 'By the way, Bunty told me Tilly had gone home, not feeling very well. What happened?'

'Believe it or not, my first patient of the afternoon was Tilly,' she said. 'I forced her to let me look at her as I know she's not been feeling too good for some time, and today was a bad day. She's had a variety of symptoms from headaches to joint pains, and she's got some peculiar red ring marks on her upper arm. I'm sure I've come across those indications before, but I just can't bring it to mind—it's rather a mystery.'

Callum leaned forward, looking interested. 'I might have an idea myself—it sounds very like something I came across when I was doing my elective studies and spent three months abroad as a student.'

'You think you know what it might be?'

'If I said Lyme disease, would it mean anything? It's the distinctive rings you mention that gave me a clue. You can contract it sometimes in this country, in heathland, but it's more common in America. Comes from tick bites and the ticks can live on a variety of animals.'

Lucy stared at him in admiration. 'I'm very impressed, Dr Tate!'

He grinned. 'I told you I was a brilliant doctor.'

She made a face at him and then clasped her hands together. 'Of course—I think it ties in! Tilly told me they'd been on holiday and had done some riding and had come in contact with deer. I've heard of the disease, but I've never come across it—a first time for everything, I suppose. We'll see what her bloods reveal...'

'If she's got it, it's usually a four-to-six-week course of antibiotics. Poor Tilly—she must feel dreadful. It takes a long time to feel better.'

'Well, she won't be coming into work for a while, that's for sure. We'll have to try and get a locum nurse to do the community work.'

He smiled. 'Let's not think about work at the moment. I've not brought you here to talk about that.'

'I know! For goodness' sake, tell me what your news is...I've been dying to know all afternoon!'

He laughed at the impatient frown on her face. 'First things first. I'm told the prawns and sole in filo pastry are a speciality here, so how about trying it?'

'Sounds delicious to me... But listen, Callum, I won't be able to eat a thing unless you tell me immediately why we're here!'

Callum quickly ordered their food. 'I meant to tell you after the meal,' he teased, then, seeing her furious face, relented and pulled the letter he'd received that morning out of his breast pocket. 'This,' he said solemnly, 'is my passport to freedom and a new life! I'm a free agent again!'

Lucy frowned. 'What do you mean?' His laugh was infectious, and then she smiled, too, uncertain why she was doing so. 'What is it? Tell me quickly!'

'It tells me that Tamsin and I are officially divorced—this is my decree absolute. Now, thank God, I can, like you, lead my own life and put the past firmly behind me!'

She gazed at him, her dark eyes wide with surprise.

'So that's it! Your marriage is over completely. No regrets?'

Callum sighed. 'I suppose I'm sorry that something that started with such high hopes ended in failure—faults, I guess, on both sides.' He took her hand across the table and squeezed it, holding her eyes with his. 'But life goes on, doesn't it? Tamsin and I made mistakes. To tell you the truth, I don't think we ever really were in love—just the idea of love perhaps. We were too young, lonely in a new country and we wanted different things from marriage—and I didn't look beyond a pretty face.'

Lucy bit her lip, not wanting to interrogate him but needing to know why he'd drifted into a relationship which sounded shaky from the start. 'And what did you want from marriage, Callum?'

'I wanted to build a home with someone I loved, have a family if possible.'

'And Tamsin didn't want that?'

He smiled rather grimly. 'Tamsin wanted some status in a new community and a meal ticket so she could indulge herself. After a year or so it was evident that marriage to a young medic wasn't going to be as glamorous or wealthy as she'd thought—and she was as bored with me as I was with her.'

'So you parted?'

'She'd fallen for the charms of a prosperous sheep farmer who lived in the area. She broke up his happy marriage and went to live with him.'

'And did she marry him?'

Callum shook his head and smiled faintly. 'That didn't work out either, and after a while his wife came back and Tamsin was thrown out—but we'd already started divorce proceedings and she met someone else.'

'And what's happened to Tamsin now?'

He was silent for a second, looking unseeingly across the firth. 'I don't know,' he said at last. 'I haven't heard anything about her for a long time.'

Lucy sighed. 'She betrayed you, Callum—just like Ben in his way betrayed me.'

They chatted easily for a while then Callum raised his glass as the waiter placed their meals on the table. 'Then let's drink to the future, sweetheart. And, for heaven's sake, let's eat this food now—I'm starving!'

As they ate, a niggle of worry gnawed at the back of Lucy's mind. She trusted Callum. She was sure he wouldn't two-time her, but was he having an affair with her on the rebound of his broken marriage? The air was balmy, but a shiver of foreboding ran through her for a second. After what he'd been through she doubted whether Callum would easily commit himself again. Was that why he had never said he loved her?

There was silence between them as they drank their coffee, and Callum looked at Lucy's profile across the table—the tip-tilted nose, the sweep of her lashes across her high cheek-bones when she looked down, the upward curve of her full mouth. She was so beautiful. He longed to tell her that he loved her totally and wanted to spend the rest of his life with her, but he hesitated. Perhaps it wasn't the right moment.

She looked so pensive that he was wary of rushing things. Someone sensitive like Lucy, who had been hurt badly before, might shy away from declarations of love, especially from someone who had only just received his divorce papers that day! Better to keep things as they were for the moment, he thought sadly.

Talk of marriage and love might frighten her off for ever.

He touched her hand across the table. 'A penny for them.' he said gently. 'You look very serious. Have I shocked you with my marriage revelations?'

Lucy shook her head, coming out of her reverie abruptly. 'Of course you haven't shocked me—I'm just sorry that you had an unhappy time.'

'Then let's go for a little walk along the shore,' he suggested, getting up from his seat. 'We'll not see another sunset like this on such an evening. I'll settle up later.'

He put his arm around her waist as they strolled down the little street, away from the bustle of the village, and down onto the shingle, their footsteps crunching into it as they walked. The sky was changing from a duck egg blue marbled with pink to blood red as the sun set beyond the mountains over the firth, and they watched it in silent awe for a few minutes.

'There's other things I want to talk about,' he murmured at last. Then he stopped walking for a moment and pulled her towards him, 'But I've got to do something first…something I've been longing to do since I saw you in this fantastic dress. Did you know it shows off all the most wonderful, sexy things about your body?'

Lucy pushed her forebodings away and laughed. 'What kind of things, Callum?' she teased.

His hand ran lightly over the fullness of her breasts and the curve of her waist. 'These kinds of things,' he said in a muffled voice as his lips made little butterfly kisses down her neck.

Then he slid his arms round her back and pulled her so close to him that they were hip to hip, the hardness and need of his body moulding into her soft form. His lips scorched her skin as his kisses became more demanding, and his hands pulled down the thin sleeves of her dress so that her breasts spilled out, the skin creamy and soft. He buried his face in them and groaned.

'Sweetheart, if the ground wasn't so hard and it wasn't so public, I don't think I could wait to make love to you...' he muttered thickly. 'Let's get home now so that I can do things properly!'

And Lucy laughed, suddenly happy again, because being made love to by Callum was out of this world. He might not have mentioned commitment yet, but she was sure he would never two-time her. She could trust him.

The journey home in the back seat of the taxi was rather a blur—a lovely haze of slightly too much alcohol and a carefree happiness that seemed to affect them both like schoolchildren, giggling together and making plans for future outings. Callum gathered her in his arms and kissed her gently as they drove up to the house—he'd made a decision. Before they went to bed tonight he would, after all, ask her to marry him, tell her he loved her to bits. He couldn't put it off any longer.

They both tumbled out of the car, Callum paid the driver and they walked up the little path, Lucy's head on Callum's shoulder, his arm round her waist. Suddenly he stopped, bringing Lucy to a halt with him.

'What the devil...?' he muttered.

Out of the shadows and into the light of the porch stepped the figure of a young woman holding something in her arms.

'Hello, Callum,' the woman said quietly. 'I thought you'd be back soon. I've brought something for you—something that belongs to you.'

Lucy heard Callum give a sharp intake of breath. His hand dropped from her waist and he stared incredulously at the woman. Then he said very slowly, his voice harsh, 'What the hell are you doing here, Tamsin?'

She stepped further into the light so that its beam fell on the bundle in her arms.

'I've brought you your son, Callum—he's three months old now and I'm not looking after him any more. He's all yours!'

CHAPTER SEVEN

THERE was a long silence between them. In the background was the distant thrum of traffic and an owl hooted somewhere in the dark. Callum and Lucy stared with a mixture of horror and disbelief at the woman who stood before them with a slightly triumphant smile on her face. In the light of the porch Lucy could see that Tamsin was beautiful, with a sheet of blonde hair framing an oval face and wide grey eyes that stared back at them almost insolently. Then the baby stirred and started to whimper and Tamsin looked down at him.

'Hush, Joe,' she murmured. 'No need to worry—Daddy's here for you now.'

Callum found his voice at last. It was hoarse and strained. 'What's happening, Tamsin—what little scheme have you got up your sleeve this time? Our decree absolute came through today—we aren't married any longer. I don't think you can get any more out of me now...'

Tamsin laughed, a tinkling noise like glass breaking. 'We may be divorced, sweetie, but you still have obligations. After all, it was never my plan to have a child—you were the one that wanted one. And now you can have what you wanted!'

Callum's breath came raggedly. 'Why did you wait so long to tell me you were having a baby? Why wait until I'd left Australia?'

'Because I didn't realise I was pregnant for some

116

months—my periods were always scanty anyway.
And then, of course, I'd met another man, in fact
we're engaged and plan to marry as soon as we can.
My fiancé has no interest in children and we travel a
lot. It would hardly be fair on the child to cart him
round with us.'

She spoke as if the baby were an inconvenient parcel that she'd prefer to leave in a left luggage office.

'So how did you find out where I was? When did
you come over?'

'Quite easy really—I asked your brother and he
told me you'd got a cosy little job up here, away from
the madding crowd. I came to London a few days ago
and now I'm staying at the horrible little local hotel
here. I won't be staying long, I assure you!'

Lucy felt as if she could hardly breathe, as if someone had hit her in the solar plexus and that any moment she might fall to the ground. This wasn't happening, it was surreal.

'Perhaps,' she managed to grind out, 'we ought to
go inside. Surely we shouldn't be discussing these
things on the doorstep.'

'As you wish,' shrugged Tamsin. 'There's a bag
there with Joe's things in—could you bring it,
Callum?'

Lucy managed to open the front door with shaking
numb fingers. Her world was tumbling down about
her. How could this be Callum's baby when he had
said that he and Tamsin had broken up when she'd
run off with someone else? That had been some time
ago...

She turned to Tamsin in the hallway. 'How do you
know he's Callum's child for sure?' she said desper-

ately. 'The baby could be your fiancé's, couldn't he? When did you meet him? What proof have you got?'

'Take a DNA test if you want.' replied Tamsin casually. 'It so happens my fiancé had treatment a few years ago for cancer that made him infertile—which suits both of us. We aren't interested in children.'

She looked at Callum and Lucy's shocked faces and shrugged. 'I'm only telling it as it is. Why pretend? I think maybe Callum's forgotten the little liaison we had when…when he tried his best to patch up the marriage after I'd left him!'

Lucy turned to look at Callum. He was ashen, a haunted look in his eyes, clenching and unclenching his fists by his sides.

'You got together again after Tamsin left you?' she asked in a hard little voice. 'You didn't tell me that…you told me the marriage was over after a year! It doesn't seem that way to me.'

Tamsin walked into the sitting room, and they followed her. She put the baby on the sofa, where he lay, blinking large blue eyes up at them and sucking his thumb.

She turned to Lucy and said mockingly 'My dear, don't tell me you believe everything men say to you—how naïve! Callum was mad about me, weren't you, darling? And you just couldn't take no for an answer when I left you! Admit that we got together again!'

Lucy stared at him stonily. 'Well—did you?'

He nodded. 'For one night…' he whispered raggedly.

'One night was enough, wasn't it?' Tamsin smiled. 'Quite a night of passion as I recall—no time to take, er, precautions. And the result, of course, is little Joe!'

Lucy looked down at the child. He was so beautiful, and undeniably like Callum—eyes the same colour of blue, hair the same shade of russet. Callum stepped forward, looking down at the baby for a minute, then he picked him up gently and cradled him in his arms, his eyes never leaving Joe's face. He put out a finger and stroked the plump little cheek, and his expression was a mixture of disbelief and wonder. Then he looked across at Tamsin very sadly.

'How could you leave him?' he asked simply. 'He's your baby—you gave birth to him. How could you go back to a country thousands of miles away, never seeing him grow up or allowing him to know his own mother?'

'I won't be miles away,' said Tamsin. 'Miles's business interests are in London. We've moved over here, so I shall be able to see him sometimes.' She shrugged, looking slightly shamefaced. 'It may be unnatural, but I'm afraid I'm not very maternal. I do love Joe in my own way, but I just can't take the responsibility on my own, and Miles is definitely not at all interested. As I said, you've always wanted a child, Callum. I know you'd be a good father—here's your chance to prove it.'

Lucy drew a deep breath, trying to fight down the nausea that suddenly assailed her, and said in a barely audible and choking voice, 'You two must have a lot to talk about. I don't think it has anything to do with me so, if you don't mind, I'll leave you to it. I'll be sleeping somewhere else for a while, so I'll just get my things.'

She nodded at them both curtly, and her heart pounding, she got ready to leave. Callum followed her out into the passage and closed the door behind him, holding her arm and preventing her from going upstairs.

'Just a minute,' he said roughly. 'You know I had no idea about this… It's come as a complete and utter shock. As you say, Tamsin and I have a lot to discuss, but you've got to believe me, Lucy, it makes no difference to the way I feel about you.'

Lucy's eyes glinted at him like hard diamonds. 'Really? You think we can carry on as if nothing had happened?'

'Of course not…I realise you must be as dumbfounded as I am. Naturally, now I'll have to think about the baby—my son—and his future, so to that extent it does put our relationship on the back burner—but only temporarily until I'm sorted out.'

He looked at her desperately, as if knowing yet dreading what her next move would be.

Lucy's glance at him was full of scorn. 'For goodness sake, live in the real world, Callum! Go back to Tamsin—it's obvious you still love her really, and now you know she's the mother of your child, well…that makes the bond so much closer, doesn't it?' Her voice quavered for a second, but she swallowed and carried on in a cold expressionless way. 'Do you think I'm a complete fool? I realise now I was just a temporary diversion, so don't think I hold any hope of us getting together again.'

She pushed passed him roughly and ran up the stairs to get her things. Bright tears filled her eyes, but she was damned if she was going to let him see how devastated she was.

Lucy sat on the edge of the bed in the little flat that adjoined the surgery and stared unseeingly in front of her. The flat smelt of a mixture of new paint and the new carpet which had replaced the old one ruined by the water. The heating was on to dry out any residual damp, but she felt cold to her bones. She seemed to be living through a nightmare. She had been so sure that Callum would never lie to her, and although he had never actually said he loved her, in so many ways he'd seemed to regard her as his. Her hope that her future was happily mapped out with a wonderful man had been shattered.

She put her head in her hands and rocked miserably backwards and forwards. How could she have been so incredibly foolish? As Tamsin had put it quite succinctly, surely she wasn't naïve enough to believe everything a man told her!

Gradually her feelings changed from bleak numbness to a cold wave of fury—fury at herself for falling so easily for Callum's charm and fury with him for using her, abusing her trust. He'd implied that when Tamsin had left him, that had been that—when in reality he had tried to renew the relationship. No wonder the man had never said he loved her, committed himself to her. He still hankered after Tamsin!

Lucy leapt from the bed and marched to the kitchen to make herself some black coffee. She was filled with an angry energy, her brain whirling with the fact that, far from being free to commit to anyone, now Callum had a child, and little Joe would be his priority now—she had seen that in the way he had looked at the child, held him so tenderly in his arms.

She sipped the scalding coffee, scowling at her reflection in the window, and muttered to herself, 'Let's face it, Lucy, my girl, you're a bad judge of character where men are concerned!'

She'd thought she'd learned her lesson with Ben, who'd flattered her into thinking she'd been the only girl in his life, had assured her that they had a future together—when all the time he'd wanted her money, an easy way to get his own business. What, she wondered bitterly, had Callum wanted from her? Someone to share his bed, satisfy his sexual needs, she supposed. And how convenient it had all been for him—no need even to cross the road or, indeed, the landing!

Thank God Tamsin had turned up when she had—before too many people knew that they were having an affair, before she, Lucy, had begun to believe that they would be together for ever. At least she could salvage a degree of dignity from the whole sordid business.

Lucy ran the cup under the tap to rinse it, surprised at how cool and calm she'd begun to feel. First things first, she decided. She would live in this little flat for the time being, leave them to live in the house until they left—because no way was Callum going to remain in the practice indefinitely. There was a three-month trial period—well, she thought wryly, he'd failed the trial and as soon as the three months was up—sooner if possible—he could disappear! And she, Lucy, wouldn't have lost anything at all—she'd be the same as she'd been before he'd stepped into her life, reasonably happy, enjoying her job and, best of all, man-free!

She went back into the bedroom and looked at herself scornfully in the long mirror of the wardrobe.

'All these clothes and new make-up did nothing to help you, did they, Lucy?' she muttered savagely. 'And I never want to see this again!'

She tore off the tangerine dress so roughly it ripped

apart. Bundling it into a ball, she threw it viciously in a heap into the corner of the room. Then she took out her old pyjamas and put them on, got into the bed and pulled the covers over her head—she knew sleep would be a long time coming.

'Dr Tate says he's got a bit of a problem—might not be in today. Could you possibly take the urgent cases? He'll be along when he can.' Bunty replaced the receiver on the phone and looked curiously at Lucy's white face. 'You OK, Lucy? You don't look very well.'

'I'm fine—just didn't sleep too well,' Lucy replied in a flat voice. 'And, yes, I'll pick up the urgent cases. Perhaps some patients could come either this afternoon or tomorrow.'

She picked up some of the morning's emails regarding patients who'd attended consultations at the hospital over the last few days and leafed through them, willing herself to concentrate on their comments rather than the 'bit of a problem' that Callum had.

Bunty looked worried. 'What about the home visits? Old Mr Macfarlane's daughter rang to say that he wasn't too good, and he's right on the other side of the firth.'

'I'll speak to Dr Cassidy,' said Lucy. 'When I saw him the other day, he did say he was feeling better and might manage one or two sessions a week if we were stuck. He might do a short surgery this afternoon.'

She sat down at the desk in her room, slightly comforted by the familiar surroundings, and switched on her computer to bring up the patients' notes. At least everything here was normal—a multiplicity of patients who relied on her to look after them, help them through various crises in their lives. She was not going to allow her own heartbreak to interfere with that.

She pressed the buzzer that activated the screen in the waiting room, telling the next patient to come through, and tried to push the events of the previous evening out of her head.

Kath Forsyth smiled shyly at Lucy as she came in carrying her little son, now a few weeks old and crying lustily. Lucy's heart jolted uncomfortably when she saw them—they brought too many memories flooding back, of that roller-coaster evening when the baby had been born and she and Callum had first kissed each other. Her instinct then had been to halt the affair before it started—she must have been mad to go against that. She pushed these thoughts to the back of her mind and held out her arms for the baby, looking down at his indignant little face, red with crying.

'And how is little Robert?' she asked, adding with a smile, 'He's certainly grown a lot and he's got good lungs, hasn't he? His weight gain's been pretty steady, too, I see.'

'Oh, yes, he's doing really well.' The girl beamed at her little son proudly. 'He's such a good baby normally.'

'Normally?' Lucy rocked the baby gently, and his hearty yells gradually began to subside.

'He just seems to have developed this horrible colic every evening after I've fed him at six o'clock. Drawing up his little knees and screaming his head off and gnawing at his hands. I've tried feeding him, but it doesn't seem to help, and then about midnight he'll fall asleep, and I'm nearly on my knees!'

Lucy smiled and stroked the child's cheek. 'The little rascal! He honestly doesn't look any the worse for it. It does seem to be a phenonemon of some young babies that they cry in the evening with bouts of abdominal pain. It could be an immature digestive system giving him wind, but it should calm down in a few weeks.'

'Is there anything I could do to help him?'

'You could try giving him a little cooled boiled water after his feed. There's also a suggestion that cranial manipulation on the baby might help—it's only anecdotal and no studies have been done, as far as I'm aware, but one of my patients says her baby seems much calmer and happier after it. In the therapy, the baby lies flat and the practitioner holds the head and "listens with fingers" to the rhythmic motions of the body.'

'I'm ready to try anything,' said Kath fervently.

'You can get some information from the receptionist about a local qualified practitioner.'

Kath took the baby from Lucy. 'I'll certainly try that,' she said, then added after a pause, 'There is something else, actually. I'd like to ask you a favour.'

'Of course—go ahead.'

'It's just, well, you and Dr Tate were so wonderful the evening he was born, coming out when the midwife was unable to come. Our family will never forget it.'

And neither will I, thought Lucy sardonically, or at least the way it ended!

'Bill and I wondered, well, we hoped…that is, we

really would love you to be the baby's godparents. Please, say yes!' she finished in an embarrassed rush.

Godparents? Did she want to do anything with that man again? The thought of being connected with him in any way now would be impossible.

Lucy forced a delighted smile on her face. 'How lovely of you to ask us, Kath. It's a great honour and, of course, I'd love to be Robert's godmother. I can't speak for Dr Tate, I'm afraid…' She wondered whether to add, I don't know how long he's going to be here, but kept quiet.

'No, no, I'll ask him myself,' agreed Kath. She beamed at Lucy. 'But I'm so pleased you can—he's a very lucky baby! I'll tell you about the arrangements later.'

She kissed the little boy's forehead and walked out briskly.

For the first time since the previous night tears welled up in Lucy's eyes. In any other circumstances she would have been thrilled that Callum and she had been asked to be little Robert's godparents, almost a precursor of any children they might have had themselves. Now the joy of doing something together had been shattered—he wasn't the man she'd thought. He'd misled her over his previous life and now his concerns must be for little Joe—she was no longer part of his future.

There was a knock at the door as she was bringing up her next patient's name and looking briefly at the notes.

'Come in,' she called, looking up.

Callum stood in the doorway—not with the usual humorous expression she knew, but with a face that was haggard and drawn. She guessed it had been a long night for him, too.

He stepped into the room and shut the door behind him.

'Lucy,' he said in a low voice, 'we need to talk. We can't leave things like this, not after what has happened. Please, come out with me at lunchtime—somewhere quiet where we can discuss the future.'

For a second Lucy felt her heart would stop. The shock of seeing him so soon was as if someone had thrown a bucket of cold water over her. Callum looked terrible and a part of her longed to reach out and put her arms round him, tell him that they could sort out this muddle together, that she loved him too much to let him go. Then a small voice inside her head said tersely, Don't become another of his mistakes, Lucy...

'What future, Callum?' she said after a brief silence. 'I don't think so. Your future lies with your little boy, I think.'

'You've got to hear me out,' he said desperately. 'We must have some sort of dialogue!'

Lucy drew a deep breath and said coldly, 'I can't think of anything we have to say to each other. I suggest you work out your three months' notice—if you want to and if you can—and then go your own way.'

He strode over to the desk and leant on it with both hands, his amazing blue eyes blazing into hers, a strand of copper hair flopping over his forehead. 'Oh, no, you're not getting rid of me that easily. You're going to listen to what I have to say. I'm not going until you've heard my side of the story!'

'I think I heard enough from Tamsin to convince

me that what you told me about the marriage wasn't quite true,' she returned scornfully.

'You've only seen Tamsin for a few minutes, for heaven's sake—surely you know me better than her?'

'I thought I did know you, Callum,' she retorted. 'I was wrong.'

All she felt now was total confusion, she reflected sadly. She didn't know what to believe. Tamsin seemed a hard, tough woman concerned only with her own needs and she hadn't taken to her at all—but that didn't make it any easier to understand why Callum had been less than frank with her about his marriage. All her mistrust of men came flooding back, all the lies and half-truths.

She stood up, two red spots of colour on her cheeks. 'I don't want to hear your explanations, Callum. I can only say that you must have been, as Tamsin said, fairly keen on her to have a little get-together again after she'd left you. What was it she'd said? "Callum was mad about me!" She's a very attractive woman—sounds like she was speaking the truth to me!'

'That's not at all how it happened,' he protested. 'The whole thing's been twisted round. If you'd let me tell you the truth...'

Lucy held up her hand, as if warding off further explanations. 'I can tell what happened, Callum. You men are all the same, aren't you? Say anything flattering to a girl to get what you want—from money to sex! You can go to hell!'

Callum's face went white and he looked as shocked as though she'd slapped his face. He stood up straight and looked down at her, a mixture of sadness and frustration in his face.

'I can't believe you think that of me,' he said quietly. 'But don't think I won't keep trying to make you understand. A few hours ago we were everything to each other...surely you aren't going to give up at the first hurdle of our relationship?'

He touched her arm gently, and she snatched it away. 'I'm not going to get embroiled in any wrangles you and your ex-wife have over a child. You call it a hurdle, I call it a mountain!'

Callum nodded. 'I don't want to involve you in that either—but you mean too much to me to let everything go without you hearing my side of the story.'

A look of incredulity and fury crossed Lucy's face and she held onto the back of her chair to stop herself shaking. 'How dare you say I mean so much to you? A funny kind of affection you feel for me when I'm not told the truth!'

He shook his head and turned on his heel and walked out.

Lucy sat down with a bump, her hands trembling. She swallowed hard to stop herself bursting into tears. She'd never thought she'd have the strength to tell Callum to get lost. As he'd said, only yesterday he'd been the love of her life and, whatever she told herself, it was impossible to switch off her feelings for him. When he'd leant over the desk and told her that she wasn't going to get rid of him that easily, she'd known she still loved him, however he'd appeared to mislead her.

The morning dragged on and Lucy did her best to pull herself into the present and concentrate on her patients. She rang up Robert Cassidy and asked if he could do a short surgery that afternoon, then at lunchtime she thankfully switched off her computer and told Bunty she'd go to do her visits after she'd had lunch.

She wasn't hungry, but she had to get out, breathe some fresh air into her lungs. She took the woodland path that led round the loch—the loch that opened eventually into the beautiful firth. The water was still and blue, and a heron flew lazily above, scrutinising the depths for food. It was so peaceful, and yet for once the magnificent scenery wasn't working its magic on her. As she walked slowly along, the picture in her mind was of a beautiful baby being held in his father's arms. She wondered how Callum would be able to look after little Joe by himself.

'If you'd like me to come in and help out with some of your surgeries, I think I could manage a few,' said Robert as he and Lucy sat in the office at the end of the day, drinking tea. 'How long do you think Callum will be off?'

'I'm not sure. He's got a few personal problems that have, er, cropped up unexpectedly.'

'That's a shame.' Robert grimaced. 'I thought we were onto a winner with him—seems such a nice stable chap. As you know, I took to him a lot. What on earth's "cropped up", as you put it? I thought he was a single man with no family ties?'

'So did I,' said Lucy with feeling. 'No point in spreading it around yet, but his ex-wife turned up with a baby. Turns out the child is Callum's and she's not prepared to look after him!'

Robert's jaw dropped and he gave a low whistle. 'You're joking! How on earth will he cope, working and looking after a child? Don't tell me we'll have to go searching for someone else after all the trouble we've had, recruiting. Of course, he may want to stay on—he'll just have to make arrangements like other single working parents, I suppose.'

Lucy put her mug down on the big desk between them. 'Somehow I don't think he'll stay,' she said briefly. 'We'll put another advertisement in some of the journals—we may have better luck this time. But I'm not going to let you do too much—you're not supposed to be at work anyway!'

'I'll do what I can. I've rather enjoyed being back in the fray for a little while—stops me thinking about my own ailments!'

He got up slowly and stiffly from his chair, obviously in considerable discomfort from his rheumatoid arthritis.

Lucy looked at him with great sympathy. 'You're still in a lot of pain, aren't you, Robert? Have the corticosteroids not made any difference?'

'They are helping. Please, don't worry, I'm not giving in yet. Still some life in the old dog!'

Lucy felt a rush of affection for her old partner as she watched him shuffle out. What he had to put up with in his agonising twisted knees and hands made her troubles seem trivial. She had her health and a good job in a place she loved, and that counted for a lot.

She started to gather up her things, and her mobile rang.

'Dr Cunningham speaking.'

The voice at the other end of the line was typically brusque and commanding—and the last person Lucy wanted to speak to at that time.

'Lucy? It's your mother here. I'd like to see you, so I've decided to come up for a few days the day after tomorrow. I need the rest, and the country air will do me good.'

Lucy's heart sank like a stone. Wasn't life complicated enough? Apart from the embarrassment of where her mother might stay—in the little house with Callum and the baby, or sharing a bedroom with her in a minute flat—she didn't really feel up to coping with her mother at the moment!!

Her mother's strident voice hit her ears again. 'Hello? Are you there, Lucy? Did you hear me? I take it that it's convenient for me to come?'

Lucy tried to inject enthusiasm into her voice. 'Yes, Mother. How lovely to hear from you. There's just one thing…you might have to share a bedroom with me.'

She could almost see her mother shuddering with horror. 'Certainly not! Fortunately I have accommodation—the hotel has had a cancellation and I'm able to stay there. I'll look forward to seeing you on Thursday. You can come to the hotel for a meal, and we can catch up on all the news, tell me what you've been doing with yourself.'

Mrs Cunningham rang off abruptly and Lucy drew a deep breath. She doubted if her mother would be pleased with any news she had to give at the moment!

She sighed and flicked a look at her watch. She couldn't worry about her mother coming just now. Some time she was going to have to go back to her own house and collect more clothes and take the cat back with her to the flat. She may as well get it over with, although she dreaded seeing Tamsin—or Callum—again.

CHAPTER EIGHT

LUCY could hear the baby crying before she opened the front door. She wondered whether to knock, then reflected angrily that it was her house, so why shouldn't she let herself in?

It didn't look like her house at all. A pram was blocking the small hallway and a huge packet of nappies teetered on the stairs. The cat was sitting on the window-sill, looking sulky.

'Hello, Daisy, are you fed up? No one taking any notice of you?' Lucy scooped the little cat up and stroked her gently. 'You can come back with me and keep me company for a while. I don't think anyone here is interested in us!'

From the sitting room the baby's cry had become an angry yell. Lucy pushed open the door and peered around in disbelief at the room. It was as if a whirlwind had swept through the house. Baby clothes covered the sofa and blankets, baby lotions and a baby bath filled up the floor area except for a patch in the middle. Kneeling down in front of a furious red-faced, kicking baby was Callum, equally red-faced and attempting to put a nappy on the baby, but with little success. Despite herself, Lucy had to suppress a gurgle of laughter at the scene. The child was so small and the man was so big, and at the moment it looked as though the baby was winning the fight!

Callum stood up and looked at her warily. 'What

are you doing here?' he said. 'I thought you had nothing to say to me?'

'I'm not here to talk,' said Lucy brusquely. 'I'm here to pick up my things and take them back to the flat.' She looked down at the kicking baby. 'You're not having much success, are you? Shall I put his nappy on for you before I go?'

Callum scratched his head. 'It's more difficult than I thought,' he said ruefully. 'It's like putting a ferret in a sack. He won't lie still. I think I'm more adept at delivering babies than looking after them.'

'Babies aren't machines, you know,' commented Lucy as she knelt down and smiled at the little baby, tickling him under the chin and admiring his chubby dimpled legs. 'Aren't you beautiful?' she whispered.

'You're very efficient,' said Callum, watching her deftly hold Joe's legs and quickly stick the flaps of the nappy together. 'Perhaps it's a gender thing!'

Joe stopped crying and gave Lucy a toothless beam, and she put him in a towelling sleepsuit, gathered him to her and cuddled him for a minute, loving the feel of his warm and solid little body against her.

'Where's Tamsin?' she said. 'Surely she hasn't gone back to the hotel and left you to deal with Joe by yourself?'

'No, she's not gone back to the hotel,' said Callum shortly. 'She's gone altogether—back to London. But don't worry—I can cope.'

Lucy stared at him aghast. 'Already? She didn't even give you time to settle in with him?'

Callum reached out and took the baby from Lucy. 'Tamsin's a law unto herself, as you probably guessed. If she's made up her mind to do something she'll do it—whatever the cost to others.'

'It's unbelievable. How could she leave this beautiful baby? I don't understand her...'

'Joe's better off without her,' said Callum, his voice rough.

Lucy shook her head vehemently. 'A child needs both parents, Callum—or at least to know that both his parents love him. Tamsin did say she loves him in her own way—which is more than I ever experienced with my father.'

They both looked at Joe, whose eyes were beginning to close as he lay in Callum's arms.

'A funny kind of love,' said Callum sadly. Then he seemed to focus on Lucy, his voice more businesslike and professional. 'By the way, don't worry about work—I'll be back on Thursday. I've found a crèche for Joe in the village. It seems very good, and I've been looking at what's for rent in the property market. There's one or two possibilities in the vicinity.'

Lucy looked at him incredulously. 'You're not thinking of *staying* here, are you?'

Callum put the sleeping baby on the sofa with cushions round him to stop him falling off, and looked at her with a wry smile.

'Why not? My work's OK, isn't it? You can't fault me on that.'

'Perhaps not,' she snapped. 'But you can't expect us to work together, not after...what's happened.'

His expression changed, his eyes holding hers for a long moment with an almost desperate appeal in them. 'I've hurt you so much, Lucy, and I'd like to put that right, but you've made it clear you don't want to hear what I have to say—and I can't force you to. At the moment I intend to work out the three months we agreed. I love it here and I want to get used to looking after Joe before I make my mind up what I'm going to do.'

'Of course you mustn't do things in a hurry,' conceded Lucy. 'Looking after Joe must be your first concern.'

She swallowed hard to remove the treacherous lump in her throat. She'd hoped, until only a few hours ago, that she had been Callum's first priority. She looked at him leaning against the fireplace, his impressive physique emphasised by the open-necked white shirt and jeans he was wearing, and wondered desperately if the attraction she felt for him would ever die down. Last night he had reduced her to a jelly when he had held her so passionately in his arms. If she closed her eyes she could smell the male smell of him, feel his rough chin on her face, his feverish lips on hers—it didn't seem possible that she could ever forget that.

Lucy shook her head helplessly. She couldn't do anything about Callum's plans for the future, but she knew she wouldn't feature in them any more. She forced herself to think of the present.

'How will you cope?' she asked. 'You can't even put a nappy on...'

Callum gave a sheepish smile. 'I'll get better at it with practice. When I was a student I couldn't give an injection to a patient—but I'm pretty good at it now!'

'What about feeds? How often does he have a bottle?'

'I won't let him go hungry, you know...'

Lucy started to gather up the scattered clothes and moved the baby bath to the wall with the lotions in it. 'Joe's got to have some routine,' she said briskly.

'I suppose he'll be having a bottle at ten o'clock? Have you got any sterilised?'

She walked through to the kitchen and bit her lip. It looked a bigger mess than the sitting room, with used bottles and the remains of a hastily eaten supper vying for space on the draining-board. She started to clear everything up and Callum stood in the doorway behind her.

'Look, I'm sorry about the mess. I was going to clear everything up when I'd got Joe to sleep, I promise you. You just caught me at an awkward moment. Twenty-four hours ago I didn't expect I'd be landed with a baby son—I suppose I haven't got to grips with it yet!'

Lucy turned round and nodded. It was hard not to sympathise with the man. Suddenly finding out you were a father—no wonder he was in shock! She looked at Callum's face with new lines of worry round his eyes, and felt a tiny stab of guilt go through her. Had he really abused her trust? Perhaps her own past had made her ultra-sensitive, too ready to be hurt and imagining deceit when none had existed.

'I'm sure you'll be an excellent dad,' she said more gently. 'Joe's a beautiful baby, and you don't need a DNA test to tell he's your child!'

'I suppose even I have to agree he looks like me,' admitted Callum.

A flicker of a smile touched his lips. No doubting that his paternal feelings had kicked in already, thought Lucy wryly. She started stacking the dirty plates in the dishwasher and put the bottles in the sterilising bowl—she was fast coming to a decision.

'Your priority now is Joe, isn't it?' she said,

drying her hands very carefully as she watched Callum's face.

'Of course—no question.'

'Then let me make a suggestion—and this is purely for Joe's good. Why don't I stay here? In my own bedroom and you in the spare room with Joe,' she emphasised. 'You're going to need all the help you can get, and as a temporary measure this might be the right thing to do.'

He laughed scornfully. 'And you reckon that would work out, do you? After what you think about me, how can we possibly live together in the same small house?' He moved towards her and looked down at her gravely. 'Joe's my responsibility, not yours. But thanks for the offer—I'll try and be out of your house as soon as I can.'

'We've got to be practical,' retorted Lucy briskly, resolutely ignoring a treacherous desire to put her arms round his neck and hold him close to her. 'It's no good being proud about this. I'm willing...very pleased to help look after Joe until...until you've found other arrangements. Besides which,' she added tartly, 'the surgery flat still seems damp to me, and I prefer my own bed! *You* certainly can't stay there with a baby, so this seems the only solution!'

He was silent for a few seconds, as if considering all the pros and cons of such an arrangement, then he said reluctantly. 'If you want to do this, I accept gratefully.' The expression in his eyes seemed tortured as he looked at her. 'It's going to be damn difficult, having you so close and not being able to...well, never mind. I promise I'll keep my distance.'

Lucy turned away from him abruptly. She wasn't sure how easy she would find it either—she would just have to keep reminding herself that he had misled her and she was not going to allow a man to ruin her life again.

'Well, then, let's start arranging Joe's possessions in your bedroom.' Then she added after a pause. 'And you can take your things out of my room and put them with his!'

As they started to put things in order, Lucy suddenly started to laugh. Callum looked up at her in surprise.

'What's so amusing?' he asked curiously. 'I didn't think you could see anything funny in this situation!'

'It's just that I can't wait to see my mother's face when I bring her here and she sees this haven of domesticity! She's coming up on Thursday and has no idea of…well, what's been happening!'

Callum looked at her sardonically as he laid the sleeping Joe gently into the cot. 'Let's hope she doesn't have a heart attack, then,' he remarked. Then he bent down and kissed his little son.

'You look well,' conceded Mrs Cunningham, having viewed her daughter critically over her glass as she sipped wine. 'You seem to have got yourself some new clothes, I'm glad to see. I hope you threw the old ones out!'

'As a matter of fact, I did,' said Lucy, enjoying her mother's look of surprise. 'A colleague introduced me to her catalogue and I went a bit mad!'

'I was going to say you never got that outfit in this out-of-the-way place—it's a desert as far as shops are concerned. You really look quite smart!'

Her mother could only give her qualified compliments, thought Lucy ruefully, but at least they were an effort to give some sort of praise.

'What's the hotel like?' she asked her mother, remembering Tamsin's dismissal of it as a 'horrible little local hotel' and suspecting that her mother's standards would be even more demanding than Tamsin's.

'Very nice indeed' was the surprising reply. 'And the most interesting people are staying here. I think I shall find it extremely entertaining!'

Lucy swallowed her amazement. 'What kind of interesting people?'

'Oh, a film crew is staying here, making some sort of film about the Highland clearances. I got talking to one of the cameramen in the hall—and do you know what he said?'

'I can't imagine, Mother.'

'He said if I wanted to be an extra I could turn up tomorrow morning very early on the film set and probably be taken on as one of the crofters! There's a bus going from here.'

It was almost impossible to imagine her mother transformed into a crofter, but Lucy was delighted that for once the spotlight was off her. She grinned rather wickedly at her mother.

'So Ballachter isn't the terribly dull place you're always telling people it is!'

'I've probably come the one week when things are happening,' said her mother dismissively. Then she leaned forward and said, 'Now, dear, tell me what you've been doing. What about the doctor you took on—the one you met at your birthday dinner? Has he fitted in well?'

Lucy sighed. She'd known the question would come up sooner or later. 'He's a very good doctor,' she said carefully, 'but, er, he has a baby now, and for various complicated reasons might not be able to stay in the practice for much longer.'

Mrs Cunningham raised her eyebrows. 'Well, that *is* unfortunate, after all the bother you had to find anyone suitable. I thought your sister told me he was divorced—in fact...' she gave a little sigh '...I did wonder if he'd be suitable for you!'

Lucy hastily took a large gulp of wine and her laughter sounded very hollow. 'How ridiculous!'

'Stranger things have happened,' persisted her mother. 'Do you see much of his family outside work? I wouldn't imagine the social life is much to write home about here.'

Lucy wondered whether to tell her mother there and then that her new colleague was actually living in her house with his three-month-old baby! She remembered Callum saying that her mother might have a heart attack if she came and saw him and Joe ensconced in the house, so perhaps she'd have to get it over with. Better for her mother to have her hysterics now than later!

'Actually, I see a great deal of him and his baby,' she began.

Mrs Cunningham was watching the wine waiter pour some more wine into her glass. 'Really? And what's his wife like?'

'She...she isn't here. Callum looks after Joe himself.'

Her mother pursed her lips. 'How very extraordinary. It must be difficult for him. Does he have a nanny?'

'There's a very good crèche in the village and the baby goes there.'

'So then he comes home in the evening after work and looks after him. That must be very hard,' observed her mother.

'Lots of single parents have to do it,' pointed out Lucy. She looked cautiously at her mother. 'Of course, it *is* hard—and that's why I help out quite a bit. In fact, he's living at my house at the moment until he can find suitable accommodation.' She added the last words in a rush, rather defiantly.

Mrs Cunningham looked in amazement at her daughter. 'What a ridiculous state of affairs,' she said at last. 'I don't think that's a good idea at all! Why should you saddle yourself with the responsibility of someone else's baby? It's bad enough when you have your own child, as I well know!' She paused for a moment, digesting Lucy's information, then sighed. 'At least you know about his responsibilities—suppose you'd fallen for him and had then found out he was a father!'

Lucy hoped her mother couldn't see the scarlet blush that crept up her face. With any luck she'd never find out how close she'd been to the truth!

Mrs Cunningham tapped her fingers on the table. 'You know, Lucy, helping to look after this man's child could curtail your social life very much. I don't want to be a nag, but time is passing, you know—the old biological clock! I should so like to see you settled like your sister with a lovely little family.'

Sometimes Lucy wondered if her mother said these things deliberately to wind her up. Surely she couldn't think they made her feel great?

'Why should you worry, Mother? You've got grandchildren anyway. I've told you, I love my work, and that counts for a lot.'

'I just wonder how you all fit in that tiny house,' remarked Mrs Cunningham as they rose from the table. 'It's a good job I'm not staying with you!'

As they walked into the lounge to have coffee, her severe expression changed to one of suppressed excitement and she waved to a man sitting in the corner surrounded by a lively crowd of people.

'That's the cameraman I was telling you about,' she whispered to Lucy. 'You know, I think I shall take him up on his suggestion to be an extra!'

'I think that's a great idea, Mother. It'll be very interesting.'

And it will stop her dwelling on my circumstances, reflected Lucy drily.

It was a funny kind of life. The evenings seemed to merge into each other as a blur of playing with Joe, bathing Joe, feeding Joe and finally putting Joe to bed. Who would have thought that one tiny human being could take up quite so much time? Lucy had a new respect for mothers of young children, and as for Tilly bringing up twins—that seemed an almost impossible feat!

Throughout it all was the strangest sensation—that this could have been her and Callum's child that they were bringing up together. Then she'd feel the dull ache of despair as reality kicked in. Sometimes she watched Callum cuddling his little son to him and turning to her in delight at his child's reactions, and she could hardly bear to think that their futures didn't lie together. But she didn't trust him any more, did she? He had told her his marriage had been a sham—that neither he nor Tamsin had been in love—and that had been a lie. Tamsin had said he was mad about her—and there was a child to prove it!

Watching Callum give Joe his bottle one morning as she ate a hasty breakfast before setting off for work, she wondered cynically if she'd been a fool to offer her help so readily. She was probably being used again by a man for his own ends. Then she sighed. If she was being taken advantage of, it was her own fault. It had been her idea to offer Callum and Joe a home—and she'd done it because she'd wanted to, because she couldn't bear to see him struggle to look after the baby by himself.

Callum put Joe over his shoulder and patted the child's back. 'By the way,' he commented, 'there's a good house come up for rent just outside the town. It's a bit bigger than I intended to lease, but it's quite a reasonable rent with vacant possession, and I've decided to go for it. Hopefully we'll be out of your way in a few days. I'll be picking up a car today as well. I can't keep asking you to take Joe to the crèche, and I can hardly take him on the bike!'

'You're going to leave?' It was hard for Lucy to disguise the dismay in her voice.

He looked at her quizzically. 'That's what you want, isn't it? We can't stay here for ever, and you've been more than generous.'

'But what about Joe? You need help with him don't you?'

'Thanks to you, he's in a pretty good routine now. I can manage in the evenings. I can even put on a nappy fairly well!'

Lucy was silent. Of course they had to leave—she and Callum couldn't live in this way for ever. Sometimes when it was time to go to bed she would feel him gazing at her. If they came close on the stairs he would stand back, determined that they shouldn't touch each other. They were tearing each other apart, she thought sadly, suppressing the powerful sexual attraction that flickered between them continually.

She looked at little Joe—the most beautiful chubby-faced baby, with such a happy disposition and who smiled with delight whenever he saw her. He could roll over on his tummy now, and copy her when she waggled her head at him. How empty the house would seem without his presence. To her consternation she was beginning to realise that she loved the child as much as the father!

'I thought your mother would have been round to see what was going on,' remarked Callum as he strapped Joe into his portable car seat before Lucy took him to the crèche in her car.

'At the moment she's occupied with being an extra in this film they're making, I'm glad to say,' said Lucy. 'But I've no doubt she'll be here in a few days...'

'I take it you told her the circumstances?'

'I told her you and Joe were here for a while.'

Callum raised his brows. 'And how did she take that?'

'I don't think she understood it too well—thought it would curtail my tremendous social life...'

He gave a short laugh. 'She's right—it does curtail your life, and that's why Joe and I must disappear.'

Lucy bit her lip. Callum and Joe finally moving out of her life was the right thing to do, but it would be like losing a part of her life. Had she been too hasty, jumping to the conclusion that he had betrayed her and used her like Ben had? With every day that passed she knew that she still loved Callum. Should she try and listen to his side of the story and see if they couldn't go back to where they'd started?

He picked up the baby seat with Joe in it. 'I'll put Joe in the car. Thanks for taking him—that will be one less thing for you to do after today. I'll see you at the surgery later,' he said.

Lucy stood up, jingling her car keys nervously. 'Callum...' she started awkwardly, 'you know you don't need to go. Joe's been moved about such a lot recently. Surely it would be better for him to stay in one place for a while.'

Callum didn't say anything as he fixed the car seat with the baby into the car. Then he straightened up and looked at Lucy rather sadly.

'Joe will get used to moving around with me—but I can't stay here any more, Lucy. You must know why—I can't take being near you and yet not close to you. To feeling your disillusionment with me, knowing what a rat you think I've been. You say I've been using you—and at the moment I feel I am. My son and I are trespassing on your good nature, when all the time there is no future for us...'

Tears welled up in Lucy's eyes and she put a hand to her mouth. 'Don't,' she whispered desperately. 'Perhaps there is a chance we could make things work after all. I've been thinking about things...'

'So have I,' he said harshly. 'I've been doing a lot of that recently—and your mother is quite right. I can only ruin your life if I hang around. You are *not* going to be saddled with the responsibility of my child—a child that means nothing to you. I do have a certain pride left.'

He turned round and went back to the house and

Lucy stood on the pavement, watching him in anguish and a growing sense of conviction—that the real reason he wanted to leave was nothing to do with taking responsibility for Joe but that he wanted out of any commitment.

'So that's it,' she whispered miserably. 'He wants out of my life, and it's a good excuse to leave me without any obligation on his part. Seeing Tamsin again has awakened old feelings—and I come nowhere close!'

She got into the car and started driving to the crèche. Joe made little crowing noises of delight—he liked being in the car. She flicked a glance at him in the mirror and said sadly, 'You mean as much as your father to me, Joe, darling—I love you to bits! But he wants out, and I can't stop him! I'm so sorry, sweetie.'

In the little kitchen Callum sat with his head in his hands, a cold cup of coffee by his elbow and an uneaten piece of toast on his plate. How could he have been such a fool as to get himself into this mess? He must have been out of his mind to allow Tamsin back that night when she'd begged him to allow her into his life again. Naïvely he'd thought it was honourable to try and save the marriage. Callum gave a mirthless laugh and ran his fingers through his hair. So much for honour! He'd known they should never have been together in the first place—all he'd wanted was for them to be free of each other.

And now he'd met Lucy…beautiful, feisty Lucy. He hadn't dreamed that he'd meet anyone again for a long time, but now he'd fallen hook, line and sinker for her, he could never, ever be selfish enough to allow her to be saddled with the responsibility of his child. She'd be happy to be with him with no strings attached, but now he had to protect her and his son.

However hard it was, he had to cut his bonds with her and leave the house, and as soon as possible the practice—for her sake and her future.

The phone rang stridently at his elbow. He sighed and picked it up.

'Dr Tate here.'

He listened to the voice at the other end of the line for a few seconds, and gave a quick intake of breath.

'Oh, Bunty,' he exclaimed in shocked tones, 'that's terrible news. I take it there's a red alert? Certainly we'll both come to the hospital if they need more medics. I'll collect Lucy from the crèche now—she's just taken my son there. Cancel all but the most urgent appointments, and perhaps you could ask Dr Cassidy if he could fill in.'

He raced out of the house, pulling on his crash helmet as he went. Starting his motorbike, he stamped on the accelerator, disappearing down the road in a shower of gravel.

CHAPTER NINE

'BUT what on earth's happened? You say there's been a serious RTA?'

Lucy fastened her seat belt—she wasn't the world's quickest driver, and had asked Callum to drive her car the short distance to Ballachter General Hospital at the edge of the town. She glanced at his grim profile as he manoeuvred the car as quickly as possible through the traffic on the main road and wondered wryly if he was even giving a thought to the conversation they'd had only a few minutes before.

She sighed, guessing that there was no room for personal feelings in this sort of situation, but the thought that he was using Joe as an excuse to leave her was like a knife turning in her heart. Why hadn't it occurred to her before that seeing Tamsin again would make him realise what he'd lost when she and he had broken up?

'Bunty said the accident had happened on the road to the moor,' Callum was saying. 'I've no real details yet, but I do know it's something to do with that film crew that's been filming up there. Apparently the A and E department's up to its ears and they're short on medical staff. I've told Bunty to ask Robert if he'd deal with a short surgery.'

'Ballachter's quite a small hospital—they aren't really geared up for a major incident. I imagine some of the cases will have to be sent on to Inverness.' said Lucy. 'I know the film crew is staying at the hotel where my mother is. She was really excited about being some sort of an extra. This will put the filming back a bit, I imagine.'

Callum swung the car into the long drive leading up to the hospital and gave a low whistle as he parked the car on a spare patch of grass. The bay in front of the entrance was filled with ambulances and police cars with flashing lights, and behind them another ambulance drove up, its siren still whining.

'Look at that,' he muttered. 'Looks like we're in for a long day.'

They leapt out of the car and ran towards the A and E entrance where a harassed-looking nurse was directing paramedics, some of them holding up drips attached to patients, others pushing trolleys at a rapid trot.

'We're doctors—been asked to help out. Where do you want us?' asked Callum.

'Go inside,' she said, waving towards the building. 'Dr Barclay's organising things in the red area—there's a lot of orthopaedic injuries.'

The scene inside took Lucy abruptly back to the days when she'd been doing her stint as a junior hospital doctor—a jumble of porters pushing patients in wheelchairs and on trolleys, nurses holding drips as they ran through to the small ops room and side cubicles, and some patients looking confused and distressed, sitting on seats by the wall.

In the middle of the confusion a small balding man with spectacles and wearing a white coat with a stethoscope dangling round his neck was frowning thoughtfully at a whiteboard and then scribbling various updates on patients. He looked up as Callum and Lucy came forward and spoke briskly to them.

'You the GPs from The Lindens? Thanks for coming. I'm most grateful. I'm Tim Barclay, the A and E consultant, and if you need help, ask me. The walking wounded and minor injuries are being triaged in the green area and we'll deal with them later.' He turned to Lucy. 'Could you take a compound fracture of tibia and fibia in the small ops room? The patient's booked for an X-ray, but he needs obs, cross-matching bloods and the orthopaedic consultant informed. There's a nurse monitoring him now.'

'What can I do?' asked Callum, shrugging himself into a white coat from a pile that were on a chair.

'We've got three critical patients in the large ops room—the team need help there in assessment. I'll come through in a minute and see what's happening.'

Callum nodded, and he and Lucy disappeared to their allotted rooms. It was like stepping back to an earlier time in her life, thought Lucy. She felt her whole system quickening as she adjusted to the heightened air of urgency mixed with the drama of serious injury when there was a major incident in Casualty—such a contrast to the slower-paced atmosphere of The Lindens.

The young man was lying on the bed in the large cubicle staring up at the ceiling, a drip attached to his arm. A familiar figure was taking his blood pressure.

'Tilly!' exclaimed Lucy in astonishment. 'What on earth are you doing here? You should be on your sickbed!'

'Heard the news on the local radio,' explained Tilly, taking the cuff off the man's arm and noting the result on a clipboard. 'I couldn't possibly stay away...they're desperate and I don't feel too bad.

This is Jake Randall—he's in a lot of discomfort with his leg. BP's 80 over 45,' she added succinctly.

Her eyes met Lucy's in a mutual understanding of the gravity of the injuries, reflected in the young man's low blood pressure, his extreme pallor and the awkward contortion of his leg with its hideous wound showing the protruding bone poking out. A huge bruise above his eye was rapidly going purple.

Lucy pursed her lips as she examined his leg carefully. 'Ooh, not very nice, Jake. But don't worry, we'll give you something for the pain. I won't say you'll immediately feel marvellous, but it'll help.' She looked at Tilly. 'We'll want detailed X-rays, including the spine. Tell them to bring the portable machine—we can't risk moving him at the moment. I'll need venous access for analgesic injection—five milligrams of diamorphine should make a difference.'

Jake groaned. 'I hope it does,' he muttered. 'It's absolute agony...'

Tilly handed her the needle and syringe. 'Jake's part of the film team,' she murmured. 'Apparently there were about fifty on the bus—twenty-five casualties.'

She disappeared to alert X-Ray that they needed the machine and Lucy flicked a closer look at Jake.

'I've seen you before,' she said as she located a vein in his arm to put in the analgesic. 'Are you staying at the Rannoch Hotel?'

'Yes, we're supposed to be here for three weeks.'

'I was having a meal there the other night with my mother, and she pointed you out as the cameraman with the film crew.'

Jake gave a weak smile. 'I *was* the cameraman,' he whispered. 'I doubt if I'll be on set now for months.

Mind you, it's the same for the others in the bus—the ones that are injured can say good bye to this project, I imagine.'

'What happened?' she asked gently as she attached a sensor on his arm to the Dynamap machine, which would give a constant reading of his blood pressure. 'Can you tell me anything about it?'

His voice was slow as if each word was an effort. 'Some young fool came round the corner the wrong way in a flashy car. The bus driver had no chance and we smashed into each other head on. It...it was horrible.'

It was a stark account, and his expression betrayed the terrible shock he'd had. It wasn't a bad thing that he should talk about what had happened, Lucy reflected. She didn't want to push him too much, but relating the story of major trauma and articulating the horror would make it easier to come to terms with later.

She patted his arm comfortingly. 'Hopefully they'll sort you out in surgery later on this morning. Try not to worry...'

He clutched her arm, his eyes haunted. 'What about the other folks on the coach—the crew and the cast? How...how is everyone? Has anyone...?'

Lucy knew what he was thinking but was frightened of putting into words. 'I don't know the extent of everyone's injuries,' she said truthfully. 'I've been told there are some critical cases, but hopefully they've got here in time for treatment.'

Then she stared at him, her mouth going dry as she was suddenly aware of the information he'd unwittingly given her. Lucy's thoughts immediately went to her mother.

'Did you say there were actors on the bus as well?' she asked with difficulty, as if her mouth were full of cotton wool. 'Does that include the people who were extras?'

'Yes, most of the extras and cast were on board, but a few of them went in a separate coach.'

Lucy closed her eyes for a second, aghast at what might have happened. It was a terrible incident anyway, but she didn't know how she could cope if she knew her own mother was involved. She hardly noticed that Tilly had come back, having made arrangements with the X-ray unit.

'They're ready to take your picture now,' Tilly said cheerfully to Jake, 'and the consultant's coming down here to assess your injuries. Don't worry—they'll handle you like delicate cut glass!'

Jake managed a weak smile and closed his eyes as the diamorphine began to give him relief from the pain. Lucy stared at him, twisting her stethoscope round and round in her hands.

'Poor young man,' murmured Tilly as she started to straighten up the room. 'He's got a long haul ahead of him—how's he bearing up?'

Lucy jerked back to the present. 'What? Oh…his BP's a bit wavery, but it's stabilised a little, and his oxygen sats are OK.' Her voice was a strained monotone, and Tilly looked at her in surprise.

'Anything wrong?' she said.

Lucy bit her lip and sat down suddenly on a chair. 'I don't know, Tilly. I just have a horrible feeling that my mother might have been on that bus. She could be lying critically injured somewhere in Casualty. I know it sounds heartless when so many other people are hurt, but I can't stop thinking about her—I really need to know where she is!'

'Oh, my God, Lucy!' Tilly bent forward and squeezed her hand. 'That's awful! Look, don't worry, I'll go and see what's happening. You've got to know…'

Tilly almost ran out of the room and Lucy took a deep breath and stood up. It was no good falling to pieces—she'd got to keep going whatever had happened. If her mother was badly injured, someone would be taking care of her. By the time the radiographer came into the room, followed by a porter pushing the equipment, she had composed herself slightly.

Tim Barclay put his head round the door and nodded at Lucy. 'Ah, that's good. Mr Randall's being X-rayed now, I see. I wonder if I can drag you away—there's a young man with suspected spinal injuries on a trolley in the small theatre. Mr Gallagher, the neurosurgeon, is coming down soon but we're very short of people on that team. Can you go and assist Dr Tate with the usual obs, cross-match blood, oxygen sats…'

Her mind in a turmoil about her mother, Lucy made her way to the small theatre. All this would happen just as Callum and she had reached the parting of the ways, she thought miserably. So many things tearing her apart.

He was bending over the patient as she came in, looking into the pupils of the patient's eyes with a torch.

'Pupils reactive,' he said, then ran a finger down one of the soles of the man's feet which curled up in reaction. 'Good plantar response as well. I don't see any obvious neurological deterioration, but perhaps we'd better book a CAT scan to be on the safe side.'

He looked up as Lucy entered the room, a flash of awareness in his eyes, as if he, too, saw the irony of them working as a team when their relationship was sinking in quicksands!

'I think you'll know this young man,' Callum said tersely. 'His name's Stevie Richards. You remember—the asthmatic patient at the country show?'

'Stevie? He was involved in the crash? Was he in the bus?'

'He was in the car that smashed into the bus.'

Callum's voice was completely neutral, but Lucy looked at him aghast for a second. Then the facts began to sink in, and a mixture of horror and anger slowly burned inside her. Why the hell had Stevie, at sixteen, been driving a car at all, let alone such a powerful one? She swallowed, trying to suppress the mounting fury she felt. If this kid had caused the accident and her mother was injured... She bit her lip. It shouldn't make a difference to her fury if her mother was involved or not—but it did anyway.

Callum flicked a look at her expression, but made no more comment. He spoke to the team grouped round the trolley.

'Right, let's get this young man on the bed. There's a suspected spinal injury, so very carefully in one easy movement. One, two, three, lift!'

Stevie didn't move once he was laid on the bed. A mask was over his face, pumping oxygen into his lungs. What one could see of his face was grey and his neck was already in a collar to prevent movement.

'What are his obs at the moment, Nurse?' Callum asked the nurse monitoring the Dynamap machine.

'Pulse 125, BP 80 over 40 and dropping.'

'Get some Haemaccel into him, pronto—he's in

shock. Is the X-ray machine around? We need detailed X-rays for all limbs, spine and neck.'

'The portable machine's just down the corridor—they've probably finished with it,' said Lucy.

'Fine. Someone direct it here. Lucy, can you give him a shot of diamorphine? Five milligrams, please.'

The team swung into action, although Lucy felt as if she was on autopilot, remembered skills coming back to her. As they worked on Stevie, concern for her mother faded slightly. This boy was the focus of their concentration, and a feeling of relief swept through the room when his blood pressure stabilised and his pulse went down.

'Hopefully this means there's no internal bleeding,' said Callum. 'I think he'll be OK.'

The boy's eyes flickered open, and he stared blankly at the team around him, blinking under the strong lights.

'Where am I?' he mumbled through the mask.

'You're in Ballachter General Hospital, Stevie. We think you've injured your spine in some way.' said Callum. 'You had a crash—remember?'

Lucy watched the boy's eyes and saw the mixture of horror and guilt reflected there. He knew what had happened, although he was probably not aware of the full extent of the mayhem he'd caused.

'Do you need me here now?' Lucy asked Callum in a tight little voice. 'I must go and find something out.'

'That's fine. I'm sure they'll need you somewhere else,' he said, then he frowned. 'Anything wrong? You look a little pale.'

She glanced back at the figure on the bed and said

in a low harsh voice, 'I'm finding it hard to maintain a detached frame of mind at the moment.'

'You mean about Stevie and his driving?' Callum sighed. 'But this is how Casualty is—our job is not to reason why and all that.'

'OK. Tell me I shouldn't moralise, but I feel sick, Callum—sick that that youth has caused so much havoc. Why the hell was he driving a car at his age, with no licence, no insurance? He needs the book thrown at him!'

Callum looked grim. 'We can't allow ourselves to think about that, can we? We're only here to mend the bodies, not pass judgement.' Then he added under his breath, 'Much as I would like to throw the book at him...'

The door to the ops room swung open and Tilly appeared. Her glance rested on Lucy and she came quickly over to her, looking grave. It was clear that the news was not going to be good, and Lucy took a deep breath as Tilly took her hands in hers and drew her to the side of the room.

'Lucy, sweetheart, it isn't brilliant news. I'm afraid your mother *was* involved in the crash...'

Lucy's throat went dry, and she felt slightly faint. 'I had a gut feeling she might have been,' she whispered. 'How...how badly hurt is she?'

'She's in ICU,' said Tilly gently. 'She's got a fractured skull...but she is holding her own at the moment. Do you want to let Callum know?'

Lucy looked across at Callum, talking briskly to the neurologist who had come down to assess Stevie's injuries. What good would it do to tell Callum? He had worries enough of his own. And anyway, he didn't want to be involved with her any more, did he?

It was better that he should be left out of her concerns now.

'I'm not telling Callum,' she said brusquely.

Tilly looked puzzled. 'Won't he want to know?'

'No, Tilly, I don't think he would…' She sighed. Why not tell her the truth? 'To be honest, he and I…well, we're going our separate ways now. I don't want to involve him.'

Tilly looked searchingly at her for a moment, then she said quietly, 'But you're still friends, aren't you? As a friend, he'd be concerned.'

Lucy looked stubborn. 'I don't want to tell him yet.' She looked pleadingly at Tilly. 'Would you come to ICU with me? I feel a bit wobbly.'

Tilly smiled. 'Of course I will, Lucy. Let's find out what's happening.'

It was quiet in the ICU unit, just a gentle whirring and clicking of machines monitoring the three patients who were lying there. Mrs Cunningham looked small and frail. She was heavily sedated and a mask over her face connected her to a ventilator to maintain her breathing. It took a lot of machines to take over from the body when a person was very sick, reflected Lucy, gazing at the myriad tubes attached to her mother—intravenous salts and glucose replacing vital bodily fluids, the ECG machine registering her heart rate and rhythm, the automatic sphygmomanometer monitoring her blood pressure.

'Poor Mum,' she whispered, taking the small hand lying on the coverlet and squeezing it. 'You and I don't get on so well…but I do love you very much.'

A tear splashed down her cheek and she brushed it away impatiently. She had to remain calm. Once she allowed herself to give way to the jumble of feelings inside her, she'd never stop crying. Tilly had only stayed a moment. She needed to get back to Casualty, and she said she would tell Tim Barclay about Lucy's mother.

'I'll be back to find out what's been happening,' she had said, squeezing Lucy's hand comfortingly. 'You know she's in good hands. Try not to worry.'

Lucy looked at her gratefully. 'You're a star, Tilly, but I don't honestly think you should be working. You aren't well yourself…'

Tilly shrugged. 'I know, I know. I shall disappear soon, but I did promise to help sort out some of the minor injuries first—I'm good at bandaging! I tell you what, I'll stay in bed for a week after this!'

Sandy, her mother's nurse on the unit, came up to check Mrs Cunningham's fluid balance and other vital signs.

'Mr Sumner's outside,' she said, referring to the neurological surgeon on the unit. 'I think he'd like a word with you—give you an update on your mother.'

Mr Sumner was a tall, distinguished-looking man with greying hair and a rather old-fashioned courtesy that inspired confidence. He held out his hand and smiled.

'Dr Cunningham, isn't it, from The Lindens Surgery?'

Lucy nodded. 'I have been to some of the lectures you've given on brain trauma,' she said. 'I almost feel that I know you.'

'Then let's put you in the picture regarding your mother,' he said briskly.

Lucy's mouth went dry. 'She looks terrible. It's not good news, is it?'

The consultant looked at her compassionately. 'We think that she was thrown forward some way down the coach and hit her head on the windscreen, I'm afraid that from the X-rays we can see she has an open skull fracture, resulting in some cranial bleeding.'

'What...what are her chances?' asked Lucy in a whisper.

'I'm not making light of the situation,' he said gently, 'but I am hopeful that your mother will recover. We'll be doing a craniotomy shortly to drain the blood and repair any damaged vessels.'

Lucy hardly took in what he was saying. All she knew was that it was serious—very serious—and that she felt horribly alone.

It was as if Mr Sumner was reading her mind. 'Have you any family you ought to inform—perhaps someone could come and stay with you for a while?' he suggested.

'I'll let my sister know. I'm sure she'd want to be here...'

She gave a sudden shiver, and the consultant patted her arm. 'Go and have a hot drink,' he said firmly. 'We'll be taking your mother down soon—we feel she's stable enough to operate on now. Try not worry.'

Try not to worry! How often had she said that to patients, reflected Lucy as she pushed money into the coffee-machine in the corridor. Those hackneyed old phrases were used to calm and reassure, but they meant nothing. She couldn't allow herself to read anything into Mr Sumner's comforting manner—her mother was dangerously ill and the next twenty-four hours would be critical.

Lucy sat on one of the spindly chairs by the machine and stared blankly into space, hardly tasting the insipid liquid in the polystyrene cup. She had never had an easy relationship with her mother, but there were reasons why she had been difficult, and had found bringing up her youngest daughter a trial. It didn't make any difference now, Lucy thought sadly. She was still her mother, she loved her, and they had been through a lot together.

She didn't notice the constant procession of people passing her in the corridor or the tall figure that stopped by her side.

'Why the hell didn't you tell me what had happened?' asked a familiar voice that made her jump, spilling some of the coffee over her skirt.

Callum was gazing down at her, his expression a mixture of exasperation and annoyance. Lucy looked away from him—the last person she wanted to see at the moment was Callum. A few days ago how grateful she would have been for his support—he would have been the rock she could have depended on. In her numb state now, after all that had passed between them, his presence only added to her distress. He dragged a chair over towards her and sat on it, leaning forward and taking her hands in his.

'You might have kept me in the picture,' he said more gently. 'I've only just heard from Tilly about your mother. Did you know she was injured when we were dealing with Stevie?'

Lucy drew her hands away and said stiffly, 'I thought she might have been on that bus. Tilly went to find out for me.'

'Then why didn't you mention it?'

Lucy looked at him steadily. 'Because it's nothing

to do with you now, is it? You don't want to be involved with me any more, so why should I bother you?'

'For goodness' sake…I don't believe this!'

Lucy stood up and he rose, too, folding his arms across his chest and looking at her challengingly. 'Why should you think I've no more interest in you, no wish to help?'

She gave a short laugh. 'Because you've made it very clear, haven't you? Remember, I've been in this situation once before—had an affair with someone who really didn't want long-term commitment. I should have learned from that so, please, don't feel you owe me anything, Callum. As you said, we're going our separate ways now.'

He stared at her, open-mouthed. 'I don't know what you mean,' he said at last. 'Surely you didn't think I could be so uncaring, so cold… Nothing could be further from the truth.'

She looked at him coolly, hoping he couldn't see or hear the painful hammering of her heart against her ribs. 'I know what you want, Callum. It's all right. I'm OK with it. But, please, don't try and involve yourself in my affairs any more. We…we had a good time while it lasted, but you're right—we shouldn't see each other again.'

He held her shoulders in his hands, pulling her towards him fiercely, so close she could smell the male scent of him, see the little lines of tiredness round his eyes. Any closer and her body would be pressed to his, her head on his chest. She closed her eyes for a moment, her imagination taking her back to when they'd been together, when every nerve end had responded to his touch, and how they hadn't been able to get enough of each other. It had been such a short time ago—why had it all gone so horribly wrong?

'Lucy, this is ridiculous,' he said harshly, giving her a gentle shake. 'Your mother's seriously ill. Please, let me help, be of some use. It's the least I can do.'

For a second she nearly gave in. The longing to feel his comforting frame against hers again was almost too much, but with sudden determination she pushed away. They were finished, weren't they—why prolong the agony?

'I don't need anything from you at all, Callum,' she shouted, then she turned with a sob and ran away from him down the corridor and out of the exit doors at the end to the car park.

CHAPTER TEN

'SURELY that's not your supper?' Jan looked disparagingly at the plastic container holding an indeterminate substance that Lucy took out of the microwave oven.

'I'm not very hungry,' said Lucy defensively to her sister. 'My appetite's gone completely, and I only want a snack.'

'I'm not surprised you've no appetite—I don't call that food! Why don't you let me cook you a nice fluffy omelette? That would be light and nutritious. You need all your strength at the moment—no good eating this rubbish.'

'Look, you're here and that's better than any food—it's done me all the good in the world,' said Lucy, giving her sister a quick hug. 'I've been able to get out of the hospital for a short time and freshen up a bit while you stayed by Mum's bedside.'

She sat down and tipped the unappetising food from the container to a plate, poking at it unenthusiastically with a fork, then pushing it away impatiently.

'I can't face it,' she sighed. 'Somehow, with Mum so ill, life seems to be on hold—until she's out of danger I can't relax.'

The two sisters looked at each other bleakly. 'She always seems so indestructible,' Jan sighed. 'Very full of her own opinions—calls a spade a spade, especially where you are concerned. Sitting by her side, watching her, she looks incredibly frail now.'

Lucy threw her uneaten food into the bin and put on the kettle. 'You must have a night off, Jan,' she said. 'I'll go and see what the latest situation is—you've been at the hospital since you arrived yesterday.'

'That's what I'm here for, Lucy—and you're the one that needs a rest. How you cope, having Callum and his baby here, I can't imagine—especially at the moment. I had no idea he had a child.'

Lucy was silent. The story was so complicated she could hardly bring herself to start telling it. All Jan knew at the moment was that Joe's mother had left the baby with Callum for 'the time being'.

'Callum's got his own place now,' Lucy explained. 'They're going to move there tomorrow—it's a house just outside the village.'

'Quite right, too!' declared Jan, sounding just like their mother. 'You've been more than kind to that man…'

'I couldn't turn him and little Joe onto the streets, could I? Every decent place in the town was full.' Lucy flicked a look at her watch. 'I ought to give the baby his teatime bottle now. I'll go and see if he's awake.'

Jan shook her head impatiently. 'Where's his father? I do think Callum should look after his own child!'

'He's getting the house sorted to move into tomorrow—he'll be back soon.'

Lucy went upstairs to get Joe down from his cot and leant for a few seconds against the bannister of the staircase. She dreaded Callum and Joe going, but in some ways it would be a relief. After her tearful exit from the hospital two days before, they had barely spoken—and she wasn't surprised. Why had she become so hysterical when he'd only asked if he could help her? She could only assume that it was a culmination of events, and her mother's accident had been the last straw.

When Callum had come home, he had looked sad and angry, but had said hardly anything to her. The atmosphere between them was tense and brittle.

'You're the only one I can talk to, my darling little Joe,' Lucy said, gazing down at the baby's little round face beaming up at her after his afternoon nap, his auburn hair sticking up like a flue brush round his head.

She picked him up and took him downstairs, cuddling him to her on the sofa, loving his sweet baby smell. He bounced excitedly up and down on her knee when she started to sing a nursery rhyme, gurgling happily.

Jan studied her sister as Lucy played with the baby. 'I think you'll miss Joe when he goes, won't you?' she remarked astutely. 'Of course, you're a natural…'

'A natural what?' asked Lucy, tickling Joe under his chin and watching him laugh.

'Mother, of course! It's a pity Callum and you haven't hit it off—I think you'd make a lovely couple. After all, he's divorced, isn't he?'

Lucy hoped her sister couldn't see the tell-tale blush she could feel spreading over her cheeks.

'Another wife is the last thing he'd want after one unhappy marriage,' she said lightly, getting up with Joe to get the bottle which had been warming in the microwave.

She settled down to feed the baby and looked across at Jan. 'You must be pretty tired—flying to Inverness from London at the crack of dawn yesterday and then spending two days at the hospital is very draining. Why don't you go and take a break at the hotel?'

Jan got up and stretched. 'Perhaps I will go and have a bath, freshen up a little. I suppose you'll go to the hospital when Callum comes back—he can babysit his own child,' she added caustically.

'Yes, I want to be there. Hopefully I'll find there's been a change for the better. The twenty-four hours after her op are very critical.'

Jan gave her sister a quick kiss and a hug. 'Poor darling, you look absolutely shattered. You must have been worried sick about her. I'll get off now, but do ring me if there's any news or if you need me.'

She drove off in the car she'd hired at the airport, and Lucy relaxed back in the chair with Joe, watching his peaceful face as he sucked happily at his bottle. It was lovely to have Jan up here with her—especially as Callum and Joe would be leaving the next day and she knew how desolate she was going to feel without them, however bad the atmosphere. Once they'd gone, she would know that things between her and Callum were finally and irrevocably over.

'You little sweetheart, I don't know what I shall do without you,' she whispered to the baby as she cuddled him to her when he'd finished his bottle. Joe was such a happy little soul and somehow her worries faded into the background when she was looking after him.

She propped him up on cushions and sat down on the floor next to him, clapping her hands and singing.

Joe chuckled and attempted to catch her fingers in his chubby little hands, making funny little babbling noises back at her. Then she caught him in her arms and swung him up in the air, and they both laughed at each other, Joe kicking his fat legs furiously. Lucy didn't hear the door open or see Callum standing watching them, but he was there for quite a long time, his mouth twisted in a wistful smile.

Eventually he gave a light cough and Lucy whirled round, the happy expression on her face dying away when she saw him. A mixture of embarrassment at him seeing her so happy with his little son and a hollow feeling of emptiness filled her, as it did every time she saw him now. She had lost her future, she thought bleakly.

'You're back,' she said tonelessly. 'Joe's had his bottle—but he still seems very lively. I think he'd like to play for a while before you put him to bed.'

'He seems to be having a lovely time with you,' murmured Callum, then added after an awkward pause, 'Am I allowed to ask how your mother's getting on?'

'She was still critical when Jan left the hospital, but I'm going over there now to find out how she's progressing.'

Callum nodded, sweeping an assessing glance over Lucy's tired face. 'Would you like me to come with you?' he asked. He put his hand up as if to stop Lucy objecting. 'I'd only act as a chauffeur. If you didn't want me to come in, I wouldn't.'

'Thank you,' said Lucy stiffly, 'but I'll be all right.'

They stared at each other for a second, their eyes suddenly locking in mutual regret. If only they could turn back the clock, thought Callum sadly. Sometimes in the last few days he had felt that Lucy was softening in her feelings towards him, beginning to realise that it hadn't been all his fault that baby Joe had come along. Given time, could she learn to trust him again? His eyes rested on the two of them, Lucy cuddling his little son to her and gazing down at him in such a loving way, and for a moment he wondered if there could be a future for them. Then he dismissed the thought abruptly. Why should she bring up another person's child?

He took Joe from her silently, and she pulled on a light jacket and went out of the house.

Mrs Cunningham had been put in a single room in the high-dependency unit, and the curtains were drawn against the bright evening light. Mr Sumner was just leaving as Lucy came in.

'Ah, Lucy, I was hoping I'd see you. Good news that your mother's been moved from Intensive Care, isn't it? We're keeping her under observation for twenty-four hours here just as a precaution, but she's breathing well on her own, and if all goes well she'll go to a normal ward for a few days.'

Lucy felt as if an enormous weight had lifted from her shoulders, and she gave him a rapturous smile. 'It's marvellous! I didn't expect she'd improve so quickly—I'm so grateful to you.'

Mr Sumner grinned. 'It feels good, doesn't it, when someone very ill starts to improve? One of the rewards of the job, I suppose. She was lucky that she was brought in so quickly and we were able to pinpoint the bleed in her brain, otherwise it could have been a very different story.'

Lucy shuddered at what might have been. 'Thank

goodness,' she murmured. 'How about the condition of the other critical patients?'

'They're coming on well. Stevie Richards is lucky—except for bad bruising, his spine escaped injury. The police have been interviewing him today, and he seems very contrite and low.'

'I should hope he is,' declared Lucy vehemently. 'I can't understand what he thought he was doing. I didn't think he was an idiot. He's not been in trouble before, as far as I know.'

Mr Sumner shrugged. 'He said it was triggered by a row he had with his father who told him he wasn't working hard enough. Stevie said he'd been up very late revising, and his father didn't believe him. Apparently in a fit of fury he rushed out and leapt into his father's pride and joy—a brand-new sports car—and roared off down the glen in it.'

'It's no excuse for causing such a terrible accident,' said Lucy, 'but his father is a very difficult man— I've experienced his rudeness. I should think Stevie finds it hard to measure up to Mr Richards's standards.'

'It's a dangerous mixture, an impetuous youth against a stubborn father,' remarked Mr Sumner. He patted her arm kindly. 'I'm so glad your mother's on the mend. I must get off now and placate my wife. We're supposed to be going out to dinner tonight and I'm late already. Don't worry, though, I'm on the end of a phone if I'm needed!'

He left the room and Lucy went to the window and drew the curtain back slightly. It was a lovely mellow evening, the low sun touching the fields of corn and golden barley. The hospital was situated on the top of a small hill at the edge of Ballachter so there was a wonderful view over the countryside to the sea beyond. It looked profoundly peaceful and Lucy drew a deep breath, filled with a sense of release after the tension of the past days.

She looked down at her mother, now sleeping peacefully, and decided to go and telephone Jan to tell her of her mother's improvement.

'It's marvellous news,' she told Jan over the phone. 'Mum's out of danger now and out of Intensive Care. She should be well on the way to recovery in a few days, and will probably be able to come home with you.'

'That's great—a wonderful relief.' said Jan. 'How are you feeling, though?'

Lucy smiled to herself. Jan hadn't missed the weariness in her voice. 'It's been a long two days,' she admitted. 'I'm going home to get some long overdue sleep now. I'll speak to you in the morning.'

She let herself into the house quietly. There were no lights on downstairs so she assumed that Callum was in bed. She walked into the little living room and sank down on the sofa, not bothering to switch on the light as the pale moon through the window was throwing enough brightness around. She felt utterly exhausted after all the emotional turmoil of the last few days, and the euphoria she'd felt earlier when she'd been told that her mother was out of danger began to evaporate.

Life had gone full circle, Lucy reflected sadly, and she was back to being on her own again after a wonderful few weeks when everything had seemed to be going so well. Soon her mother and sister would be back in London and Callum and little Joe would have left. Desolation and loneliness began to overwhelm her, and tears of self-pity edged their way down her cheeks. She clasped her arms round her body and rocked backwards and forwards, trying to calm herself. At first she didn't hear Callum's voice, but gradually it impinged on her consciousness and she looked across the room, startled. He was standing by the small armchair.

'What is it, Lucy? Why are you so upset? I just rang your sister at the hotel and she tells me your mother's doing very well…so what's the problem?'

Callum's voice was hesitant but gentle. Perhaps he's frightened I'm going to get all hysterical again, thought Lucy wryly, dabbing at her eyes with a handkerchief. She was too tired to get worked up, too tired even to wonder what he was doing in the room.

'It's reaction, I suppose,' she said. 'I've been thinking how near we came to losing my mother—I've been on a knife edge, thinking she was going to die. We don't get on with each other really, but perhaps I've been given another chance to wipe the slate clean and try and see eye to eye with her.'

Callum switched on the light and Lucy blinked up at him. He looked strong and lean in his dressing-gown and, though she dared hardly admit it to herself, very sexy! Even now, she thought bleakly, when he's about to leave, I can't get the damn man out of my system!

'Mrs Cunningham isn't an easy woman, I guess,' said Callum gently, sitting down next to Lucy. 'She seemed to be rather critical of you a lot of the time…'

Before the accident Lucy might have agreed with him. Now she felt defensive and rather too much aware of Callum's closeness to her. 'It wasn't really her fault—she'd had a hard time of it since her first husband died.'

'And then her second husband left her—your father?'

'He was a rat,' said Lucy with feeling, 'but I think my mother always felt that if I'd been a boy he would have stayed. He wanted a son and so did she!'

'That's ridiculous, and you know it. She's just trying to shift the blame,' said Callum forcefully.

'Nevertheless, he hurt her badly. Apparently he made such a fuss about wanting a boy to carry on the line—like royalty! My mother couldn't have any more children after me and she blamed that for him leaving.'

'Did he get married again?'

'Yes.' Lucy looked sadly at Callum. 'He had another family—two boys. He never came and saw me again.'

'That was a quite a long time ago, wasn't it?' said Callum gently. 'Your mother should have moved on from there—blaming you for an unhappy marriage is grossly unfair.'

He got up from the sofa and looked at her wan face. Then he said briskly, 'Why don't we have a little whisky and cocoa? I gave it to you once before, and it seemed to do you good!'

Lucy gave a shaky laugh. 'I don't know…seems a funny thing to do when we're going our separate ways!'

'It seems to me just the right thing to do. I think it would be good to toast the future—look back fondly on the past! What do you think?'

Why not indeed? reflected Lucy. Perhaps it was a good way to say goodbye—a friendly drink before they went to bed. They wouldn't have time tomorrow. She took the mug he offered her a little later and sipped the scalding liquid gratefully, feeling the whisky hit the back of her throat.

'How did you know I was downstairs?' she asked Callum. 'I thought you were in bed.'

'I was sitting in the chair here, thinking. I needed some time to myself,' he said cryptically. He stopped and swirled the hot liquid round in the mug, watching the steam rise from it. 'I began to wonder if I was in my right mind,' he added slowly.

'What do you mean?' Lucy looked at him blankly.

Blue eyes looked at her piercingly. 'Can't you guess, Lucy?' He got up restlessly and walked up and down the little room. 'I mean that I must be mad to leave you. I thought I was doing you a favour, getting out of your life. But this evening I've begun to realise how hard it's going to be to exist without you. I don't know if I can do it!'

The expression on Lucy's face was cool, although a little shiver of excitement had begun to flutter somewhere in the pit of her stomach.

'What's brought this on?' she asked, suddenly finding it hard to breathe. 'It's hopeless to think we have any future together after all you said to me...all I said to you. We both had valid reasons for calling it a day, didn't we?'

Callum sat down beside her and leant forward, holding his mug so tightly his knuckles turned white. 'Joe and I leaving in the morning seemed to concentrate my mind,' he said haltingly. 'I...I've been watching the way you've looked after Joe. You're wonderful with him...'

'So you want a mother for your child? You think

I'd fit the bill as it were—is that it?' Lucy's voice was bitter, aware that she was forcing herself to be harsher and crueller than she'd intended to be.

Callum shook his head and looked at her aghast. 'You know that isn't what I meant,' he growled, anger tightening the muscles round his mouth, making him look hard. He checked himself for a second and put down his mug. 'What I meant…what I *know*, Lucy, is that you love Joe. I can see it in your eyes when you hold him and play with him. You love him to bits, don't you?' His voice softened. 'And he adores you, too…'

'So where does that leave us?' asked Lucy. 'It's true that I do love Joe—I'll miss him so much when he goes—but, nevertheless, why should I be a glorified nanny? We're still as we are, aren't we? You really wanted to be with Tamsin, but she dumped you. I don't want to be with someone because they find it convenient, or to be second best…'

Callum made a small exclamation and put his hand over her mouth for a second, looking deep into her eyes with a pleading intensity.

'Stop it, Lucy—stop it! For God's sake, it wasn't like that at all with Tamsin and me. The truth is that she did come back for one night after she'd run off with some man. She'd regretted her impulse, thought I was a better bet after all.'

'So Tamsin was the one who made all the running?' Lucy looked at him cynically. 'That wasn't what she said…'

'You've got to believe me,' Callum said fiercely. 'She just turned up out of the blue. I thought we should give the marriage one more try. After all, we had made vows to one another once, although I knew we were totally incompatible. It was only the next morning that she admitted she was already engaged to another guy. I realised then that she didn't care a damn what she did with people's feelings. All she cared about was herself.'

His face looked haggard and intense, little lines of weariness etched round his eyes, and Lucy knew he was speaking the truth. He was not the sort of man to give up on something lightly—as he'd said, he'd tried to keep his marriage vows although his wife had long abandoned them.

She shook her head incredulously. 'So Tamsin came back to you for the night and she was already engaged? What did she hope to gain from that?'

'I don't know,' sighed Callum. 'I can only speculate. I think this man had everything she wanted except one thing...'

'What was that?'

'He didn't have much interest in the sexual side of things—Tamsin would miss that,' said Callum drily. 'It wasn't until the morning that she revealed she was engaged and I made it clear I wanted nothing more to do with her—ever. She appears to be with him still, so I guess she's made the best of things.'

Lucy was silent for a moment and Callum took her shoulders and turned her round to him, forcing their eyes to meet. She stiffened and tried to draw back, knowing that if she allowed herself to respond, her body would betray her. She could almost feel herself curling into him, her head against his chest, hearing his heartbeat. He would not be able to mistake that message if she gave in. Her brittle façade would collapse.

He gripped her more firmly, his voice harsh. 'Don't

you believe me? You could never be second best for me. The night we had a meal together by the bay I was going to tell you when we got home that I loved you, wanted to marry you...but I was just too late, wasn't I?'

He put his hand round the back of her neck and pulled her head gently towards him. 'Am I too late now, sweetheart?' he whispered. 'Too late to make up for lost time?'

His face was so close to hers, his dark-flecked eyes gazing into her very soul. Then very gently and tenderly his mouth brushed her lips, and she could resist no longer. Her arms wound round his neck and she opened her mouth to his, every nerve end responding to his touch.

He drew back for a minute and murmured huskily, 'I do love you so very much, Lucy. Don't let's throw it all away. Dammit, I've waited thirty-four years to find the right woman. I can't wait until I'm nearly seventy to find another!'

A huge surge of happiness began to engulf her and she whispered, 'What are you saying, Callum...that you want to marry me?'

'I didn't want to at first—I thought I'd never want to get married again.' He stroked a tendril of hair back from her face and chuckled. 'How stupid I was! Gradually I began to realise how perfect you are— that I would never find anyone like you again in my life. We're just right for each other, you and I!'

Those tantalising lips trailed butterfly kisses down her neck and Lucy allowed the old incredible excitement to flood through her, as if every erogenous zone had been switched on. His kisses became more passionate, plundering her soft mouth, his hands stroking her body gently but relentlessly. She gave a little sigh, knowing she would surrender but also secure in the knowledge that Callum truly loved her.

She smiled up at him. 'Here's to the rest of our life, then...'

EPILOGUE

IT WAS a soft late summer day with a haze lying over fields that led down to the sea, and the sweet smell of new-mown hay drifted across the garden. A perfect setting for a perfect day, thought Lucy, happy little bursts of excitement exploding inside her as if butterflies were fluttering inside her stomach. Her gaze swept round the assembled guests and rested on her mother, sitting under a parasol like a queen bee. Two weeks ago Lucy couldn't have believed that this would ever happen—a party would have been the last thing on her mind.

'You know, it is really very sweet of you to hold a party before we go back to London,' said Mrs Cunningham with unaccustomed charm. 'And such a lovely day. The view from here is spectacular—you wouldn't get this in London!'

Lucy's eyes met Callum's in mutual amusement—her mother seemed to have mellowed rather since the accident!

'So you admit that Ballachter does have some good points,' teased Lucy. 'I didn't think you'd find anything in its favour—especially when you were nearly killed up here!'

Her mother smiled. 'I hope I'm not that biased. And I have a lot to be thankful for as well—excellent medical attention for one thing.' She looked across at Mr Sumner, the surgeon who had performed the craniotomy. 'I can't tell you how grateful I am to you, Mr Sumner...'

He smiled and raised his glass to her. 'It's lovely to see you looking so well. Lovely to be invited to this party!'

'I really believe you are happy here, Lucy,' admitted her mother. 'Now I've seen the place and got to know some of your friends, I realise there's a lot to be said for it. I just hope that some time Mr Right will come along for you!'

'Yes, Mother, that would be nice—if it ever happens!' Lucy suppressed a giggle, anticipating the astonishment her mother was going to experience when she realised just why the party was being held!

The excitement of the past week churned inside her—after all that had happened it was hard to believe that Callum and she were together at last. She looked across at him proudly, thinking how well his light blue jacket and cream trousers suited his tall frame, how he stood out amongst the guests—and that, incredibly, he was all hers!

Mrs Souter, an elderly patient of Lucy's, had come with some friends to help out with the catering, and Tilly, her husband and twin sons were amongst the guests. Nobody except Tilly was in on the secret that Lucy hugged so happily inside her.

Tilly came past as she refilled guests' glasses with champagne. She drew Lucy to one side and said in an exasperated whisper, 'When are you going to tell everyone the news? I can't wait to see their expressions when they find out!'

'Soon—very soon. I'll just go and get Joe,' said Lucy. 'He's got to be in on the excitement, too!'

She went upstairs to where Joe had been having a

nap in his cot and gazed down at him lovingly. Whatever arrangements were made for him in the future to see his real mother, she, Lucy, would always be there for him. Joe meant as much to her as if he were her own child. And, of course, he was part of Callum so how could she not feel love for his little boy?

She picked him up and went outside. Everyone knew by now that Callum had his baby son living with him, but nobody except Tilly seemed to be aware that Lucy was in any way part of Callum's life now. As far as the village was concerned, Lucy was a colleague who had merely been a support for him in time of trouble.

Callum was talking to Kath and Bill Forsyth who had brought their baby son with them. He turned to Lucy and smiled at her.

'I was just telling Kath and Bill how delighted I'd be to be Robert's godfather. I shall never forget that he was born on the first night I came to Ballachter, so he's a very special baby to me. Perhaps we could organise a double christening and little Joe could be christened at the same time!'

The young couple laughed. 'Great idea,' enthused Bill. 'We could certainly organise that.' He looked round at the assembled people. 'It's very kind of you to invite us to celebrate Mrs Cunningham's recovery—you must be so relieved.'

'I'm all for celebrations when something wonderful happens,' said Callum. He winked at Lucy and then stood up on a chair and clapped his hands, calling for silence. Everyone turned round expectantly.

'Ladies and gentlemen, as you know, we are here today to celebrate. The first thing we're celebrating is the fact that Lucy's mother has made a marvellous recovery, and for that we're all profoundly grateful...'

There was a general murmur of assent, and some people started clapping. Callum held his hand up.

'I've not quite finished yet.' He smiled. 'There's something else I'd like to celebrate—and I think Lucy would join me in this. You see, something has happened that neither of us thought would take place— in fact, we both thought my stay at Ballachter had come to an end and it was time to move on... But we were wrong.'

He looked across at Lucy holding his son and got down from the chair so that he could walk over to them. He took the baby from her and put his arm round Lucy.

'Lucy and I have something to celebrate ourselves. You see, folks, we've discovered that we deeply love each other. We're going to get married, and we want you all to be part of the wonderful day that she and I became engaged! Please, let's drink a toast to the future!'

After a general intake of breath and a stunned silence, there was a small roar of amazement. People turned to each other as if to ask if they'd heard correctly, and then a storm of clapping filled the garden.

Mrs Cunningham took Jan's arm and walked slowly across to Callum and Lucy.

'Am I dreaming?' she asked in a dazed voice. 'I thought Callum said you'd got engaged!' She looked at them searchingly as if suspecting a hoax.

Lucy laughed and leaned forward to kiss her mother on the cheek. 'You're not dreaming,' she said, 'It's quite true! We're going to get married in the autumn!'

'But you told me you didn't need to get married—you had your work... Why didn't you say anything to me?'

'Because...I don't think we really knew what we wanted until a few days ago.'

Suddenly Mrs Cunningham started to cry, dragging a handkerchief out of her handbag and pressing it to her eyes. 'I'm sorry,' she said indistinctly. 'I'm just so happy!' She put her hand on Lucy's arm and looked into her eyes for a moment. 'My dear Lucy, it's hard for me to admit, but I've been doing a lot of thinking since my brush with death, and the fact is, I know I've been rather critical of you in the past, but all I've ever wanted was for you to be happy, to have someone to cherish you. I've learned that that is very important.' She looked rather wistfully at them both for a second, then seemed to pull herself together, smiling happily through her tears. 'And I'm sure that with Callum you'll be very happy indeed.'

Lucy hugged her mother. 'Thanks, Mum, I know I will.'

Mrs Souter was passing with a plate of canapés. 'I could have told you this would happen,' she said triumphantly. 'Didn't I say so the day before Dr Tate came and I learned that he wasn't married? I can remember almost the precise words I said to Dr Lucy when she came to visit me. ''Given the right circumstances and a very pretty lass, most men succumb!'''

Callum held little Joe tightly to him and looked down tenderly at Lucy. 'How right you were, Mrs Souter—how right you were!'

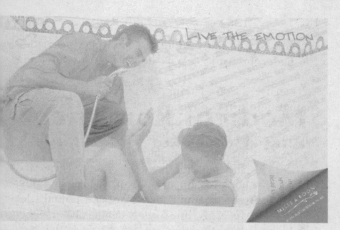

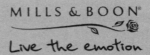

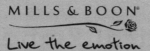

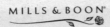

Coming Home for

Christmas

Three brand-new seasonal romances

HELEN BIANCHIN   LUCY GORDON   REBECCA WINTERS

On sale 7th November 2003

Available at most branches of WHSmith, Tesco, Martins, Borders,
Eason, Sainsbury's and all good paperback bookshops.

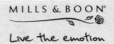

MILLS & BOON®
Live the emotion

PENNINGTON

Catherine George
PENNINGTON
Reform of the Rake

MILLS & BOON

BOOK FIVE

Available from 7th November 2003

*Available at most branches of WHSmith, Tesco, Martins, Borders,
Eason, Sainsbury's and most good paperback bookshops.*

4 FREE

books and a surprise gift!

We would like to take this opportunity to thank you for reading this Mills & Boon® book by offering you the chance to take FOUR more specially selected titles from the Medical Romance™ series absolutely FREE! We're also making this offer to introduce you to the benefits of the Reader Service™—

★ FREE home delivery
★ FREE gifts and competitions
★ FREE monthly Newsletter
★ Exclusive Reader Service discount
★ Books available before they're in the shops

Accepting these FREE books and gift places you under no obligation to buy, you may cancel at any time, even after receiving your free shipment. Simply complete your details below and return the entire page to the address below. *You don't even need a stamp!*

YES! Please send me 4 free Medical Romance books and a surprise gift. I understand that unless you hear from me, I will receive 6 superb new titles every month for just £2.60 each, postage and packing free. I am under no obligation to purchase any books and may cancel my subscription at any time. The free books and gift will be mine to keep in any case.

M3ZEE

Ms/Mrs/Miss/Mr ....Initials.....................................
BLOCK CAPITALS PLEASE

Surname ....

Address ....

....

....Postcode.....................................

Send this whole page to:
UK: FREEPOST CN81, Croydon, CR9 3WZ
EIRE: PO Box 4546, Kilcock, County Kildare (stamp required)